Saracen!

Blaine Saracen has returned home to Texas to find his parents dead and his sister taken by Black Ted Allen. So begins a long quest to find his sister.

In the course of his journey, Saracen is caught up in a bloody showdown, having saved the lives of two United States marshals, then is given the job of transferring a prisoner to Fort Smith.

While Saracen is gone, Allen reappears with a vengeance, killing and robbing. But the outlaw's luck runs out when he is captured, only to be freed while being transported for trial. Though once Saracen gets word of it, nothing will stop him from getting the man who killed his parents and took his sister.

Saracen!

Brent Towns

A Black Horse Western

ROBERT HALE

© Brent Towns 2019
First published in Great Britain 2019

ISBN 978-0-7198-2989-5

The Crowood Press
The Stable Block
Crowood Lane
Ramsbury
Marlborough
Wiltshire SN8 2HR

www.bhwesterns.com

Robert Hale is an imprint
of The Crowood Press

Typeset by
Derek Doyle & Associates, Shaw Heath
Printed and bound in Great Britain by
4Bind Ltd, Stevenage, SG1 2XT

CHAPTER 1

Arizona 1879

The sickly-sweet stench of burning flesh was mixed with thick, dark woodsmoke that rose into the otherwise clear Arizona sky. Blaine Saracen stared numbly down at the flint-headed arrow in his right hand and then back up to survey the chaos before him. What remained of the Mortimer homestead was little more than a flaming pyre, and he was sure that amongst those flames lay the bodies of Henry and Alice Mortimer.

Saracen wrinkled his nose and removed his black, low-crowned hat. He sleeved sweat from his brow and replaced the hat on his head, pushing it down over dark hair. His blue shirt suddenly felt too hot, and he wished he could take it off.

The six-foot-three scout in his late twenties, with broad shoulders and narrow hips, figured that the Chiricahua Apaches had hit sometime around daybreak while the Mortimers were still asleep. The corral was empty, which meant that the horses had been taken. If Saracen remembered rightly, when he'd ridden through three days before, Henry Mortimer had four horses in it, one a tall buckskin which the man seemed to prize above all else.

To the right of the corral stood a large barn, and for some reason its plank sides were totally untouched by the flames. Beyond it was a small spring from which the Mortimers used to draw all their water.

A flurry of feathers in the centre of the homestead yard drew the scout's attention. Vultures were fighting over a scrap of meat from what had once been the Mortimer's hired hand, a middle-aged man named Prentiss.

Saracen spat on the dry earth at his feet. The way the day was shaping up, he wouldn't be surprised if the globule sizzled and faded away immediately.

About to turn from the scene before him, the hairs on the back of his neck stood up, telling him that he was being watched. With well-trained eyes, he stared out over the engorged birds to the wall of mesquite beyond.

He saw movement. Not much, just a flicker of dark through the brush, and then the light was back.

Saracen dropped the arrow and took up his Winchester '76 in both hands instead of just the left. Turning his back, he walked steadily towards his red roan.

A bird call sounded to his left, followed by two more. Silence, and then another.

'Christ, Blaine. What have you gone and got yourself into? Should have stayed in Texas.'

It was normal for Saracen to admonish himself when his stupidity left him in tricky situations. This time he'd be lucky if it didn't get him killed.

He shook his head, knowing that the secret of a good defence is a good offence. Well, he sure as shit wasn't going to wait for them to come to him.

It was a quail that triggered it, disturbed in the clump of mesquite to Saracen's right, and with a cry of alarm, the bird erupted skywards, its wings beating a furious rhythm in its panic to get away.

Saracen swung around and brought the .45-70 up and fired at the mesquite. The slug ripped harmlessly through the brush and the vultures took flight. He levered and fired twice more and heard a yelp. A half-naked figure exploded from the screen, a battered old Spencer carbine in his hands.

Saracen fired again, and the Apache collapsed in a heap on the ground.

An ear-piercing shriek sounded from Saracen's left as another Apache leapt from behind a clump of rocks where he'd been sheltering. He, like the previous warrior, had a naked torso and wore a breechcloth and leggings. About his head was a faded red bandanna, and his hands brought up a bow, an arrow nocked and ready to fire.

The warrior released the arrow just as Saracen went down on one knee, the deadly missile passing harmlessly over the scout's head. The Winchester in Saracen's hands roared once more, and the Apache cried out then gasped at the splash of red that appeared on his chest, left of centre.

7

A third Apache emerged from behind a clump of rock and cactus beyond the corral. He, like the first one, had a gun – but this one Saracen recognized: it was the Yellow Boy Winchester owned by another of their scouts, Crowe. He'd know the weapon anywhere. The scout had sat polishing it for many hours late into the evening, but had disappeared a week before.

The warrior fired before Saracen could lever a fresh round into his own Winchester's breech. The snap of the slug caused the scout to duck instinctively. He cursed under his breath and brought the weapon to bear. The hammer fell on a live round and the .45-70 roared into life.

Punched back by the hammer blow, the Indian dropped the rifle. His arms flailed in useless wild motions before he toppled sideways on the solidly packed earth of the ranch yard, until his head came to a stop when he could go no further.

The fourth and last Chiricahua warrior material-ized from the thick smoke of the fire, no more than ten yards from Saracen. A cold hand seemed to touch the scout and a chill ran down his spine. There was no way that he could get the Winchester around and fired before the Apache killed him with the loaded bow he had drawn back and centred on him.

Saracen braced himself for the burning pain he knew would come with the flint head's passage as it smashed and tore its way into his body. With any luck, it would kill him outright and he'd feel nothing.

Instead, the Apache's head snapped back at the sound of a gunshot, a mist of blood and gore spraying from the back of his head as the bullet blew out a large chunk of the warrior's skull. The bow dropped from lifeless fingers, and the Apache fell to the ground. Saracen stared at the prone form.

'My great Aunt Fanny's ass, Saracen,' a voice cackled from behind him. 'That son of a bitch had you dead to rights. Are you slowing down or just getting careless?'

Saracen turned and stared at his saviour dressed in stinking buckskins. The little man had white hair and a nut-brown face with deep lines that seemed to have been carved there over the thirty years he'd been scouting for the US Army. His name was Tyrell Banks, and like Saracen, he was a scout out of Fort Collins.

'I had him covered,' Saracen growled.

'Covered? Hell, boy, that bastard would'a stuck you good with that arrow he was aiming to pin you with.'

Saracen stood erect; his frame cast a long shadow no matter where the sun was. He reloaded the Winchester while scanning the surrounding rock-covered ridgelines. They looked clear, but one couldn't be sure. There could be a dozen Apaches hiding behind any great slab of granite out there.

Banks looked over the dead Indians. He picked up the Yellow Boy, and when he stood up, he inspected it, then said, 'Chalipun ain't one of them. I figure they could be a different band.' He held out the Yellow Boy for Saracen to see. 'You see this?'

Saracen grunted and rubbed at the dark stubble on his square jaw. 'That's all we need. Another bunch to go along with the thirty or so that jumped the reservation.'

That was why they were out there. Chalipun had left San Carlos with thirty warriors, and word had it that he was headed for Mexico. Most likely the Sierra Madre Range where many other Chiricahua sought refuge. 'B' troop had been dispatched from Collins to intercept them. Unable to locate them just yet, it was fairly obvious to see where they'd been.

'B' troop was under the watchful eye of a new captain by the name of Alexander Peters. He was from back east, and as far as Indian fighting went, was as green as they came.

Brown eyes stared pointedly at Banks. 'They took the children.'

'Shit! Poor little bastards. You're sure?'

'Yeah.'

'This'll put a bigger burr under the captain's saddle. I wonder whose feet he'll lay the blame at this time?'

Banks was right. From the beginning of this patrol, anything that had gone wrong, through no fault of anyone's except for the commanding officer, had been blamed on the troop.

'I don't give a damn who he blames. All that matters is that we get those children back.'

Banks nodded. 'I agree.'

The steady rumble of hoofbeats sounded in the distance. It wasn't long before the column of cavalry appeared. 'B' troop was down in numbers, but even so, still boasted fifty mounted men. Most were veterans, which was why they'd been chosen for the task at hand.

Captain Peters brought the small column to a halt and dismounted. He approached the two scouts, along with a young lieutenant named Walker, and a burly sergeant, an Irishman who claimed the name of Michael O'Rourke.

'What happened here?' Peters growled.

The captain's baby-faced features were burned red by the harsh Arizona sun. Saracen figured that if the ignorant pup stayed alive long enough out in the desert, the face would eventually lose its innocence and turn the same shade of brown his was. A great pity that it wouldn't make him a better officer, however. He might just make it if he listened and learned from O'Rourke. Still, he always rubbed the scout the wrong way.

Saracen said dismissively, 'What does it look like?'

Peters' eyebrows knitted. 'I asked you a question.'

It was Banks who answered. 'The damned Apaches hit the place. Which means we are now behind them instead of where we should be.'

The captain turned to the young lieutenant. 'Put Farmer on a charge. If it weren't for him, we could have been here to stop all of this.'

'Yes, sir.'

'It ain't Farmer's fault his horse went lame, Captain,' O'Rourke said in a quiet tone.

Saracen looked over at the column and saw the two troopers who were riding double.

He settled his gaze on Peters. 'This happened early this morning. There's no way you could have stopped it. So don't go blaming one of your men for something

11

that was beyond his control.'

Peters' gaze hardened. 'You stick to your scouting, Mr Saracen, and leave my men to me.'

'Christ, Banks. Tell him the rest before I forget myself and take his stiff collar and choke him with it.'

The old scout informed Peters of the facts, including the missing children. A look of panic became etched on Peters' face. 'Lieutenant, get the men ready. We need to get after Chalipun before he gets into Mexico. If we push hard enough, we should catch them before they cross.'

Saracen whirled around and was about to say something when Banks cut him off. 'Maybe you should let one of us ride on ahead, Captain. We'll get the lay of the land. Remember, there's another band of Chiricahua out there now. The same ones who most likely done for Crowe. What do you say?'

For a moment, Saracen thought Peters was going to consider it. Instead, he shook his head. 'There's no time. I want to be on their tail before dark.'

Saracen turned away and began walking towards his horse.

'Where do you think you're going, Mr Saracen?' Peters called after him.

'To try and stop you from getting all your men killed,' Saracen threw back at him over his shoulder. 'Banks, make sure he don't do anything foolish.'

'Where you headed?'

'The only water between here and the border.'

'Chiricahua Springs?'

'Yeah, Chiricahua Springs.'

Blaine Saracen lowered his field glasses and retrieved a dark blue bandana from his pocket, wiping sweat from his face, his eyes burning from the salty droplets. He then placed the glasses back to his eyes and scanned the Godless wastes before him. Out there somewhere were thirty Chiricahua Apaches and two white children taken after the raid on the Mortimer farm.

He'd tracked them here. Chiricahua Springs. A waterhole the Apaches used often when crossing the border into Mexico, or vice versa.

Saracen had been here before. The spring was surrounded by large boulders, saguaro, prickly pear and mesquite, which made it a perfect hide and ambush site for the Apaches led by Chalipun.

'I don't like it, Captain,' Saracen said quietly to his commanding officer. 'We could be riding into a trap.'

Captain Alexander Peters couldn't hide the contempt on his face as he growled, 'Mr Banks, would you mind repeating what you told me?'

'I said likely as not they'll be gone by now.'

'Come on, Tyrell,' Saracen snapped. 'You know there's a good chance they're in there waiting.'

'There's that,' Banks agreed. 'But they have to know we're coming. I reckon they stopped for water and skedaddled out of there.'

Saracen couldn't believe what he was hearing. He shifted his gaze to O'Rourke. 'What about you, Irish? You know Apaches just as well as anyone.'

The sergeant nodded. 'I think a looksee before we ride on in there might be wise, sir.'

'This isn't a democracy. I give the damned orders here. Now, Mr Banks, you said something earlier about there being another way out of there. Yes?'

'On the other side.'

Peters nodded. 'Right. Sergeant O'Rourke, since you are lacking the fortitude. . . .'

'Hang on a damned minute, Peters!' Saracen exploded. 'I've known O'Rourke for a long time. And for you to insinuate that the man is a coward is a gross disrespect. All he's trying to do is save his men from getting killed. Which you seem to have no consideration for.'

The captain gave Saracen an icy stare, and without taking his gaze from him said, 'Take ten men with you, Sergeant. Proceed around the spring, and in case the Apache are there, you'll be in position to cut off any escape. Take Mr Saracen with you.'

The scout shook his head. 'Come on, Mike.'

O'Rourke followed him and once they were out of earshot, said, 'Thanks, Saracen.'

'The damned fool was out of line. As it is, I've got a bad feeling about it all. How many married men are with "B"? I know of three.'

'Six.'

'I don't want to tell you what to do, Mike, but start with them.'

'Ahead of you on that one,' O'Rourke paused. 'If you're right, Saracen, that ignorant son of a bitch is going to get a lot of my men killed.'

14

'Not if I can help it, Mike. Not if I can help it.'

Banks knew they were in trouble the moment the troop dismounted at the far end of Chiricahua Springs. All the signs showed that the Apache had passed through the clumps of boulders. But as he looked around, he found that their trail vanished, swept clean by mesquite branches.

'Christ,' the old scout murmured aloud.

'What's wrong?' Peters asked.

Banks ignored the question and let his gaze wander over the surrounding landscape. Tall saguaros stood on the ridges like an army of soldiers around the spring, standing guard over the precious water source. His eyes searched for something. Anything! Then he admonished himself again for being a fool and not listening to Saracen.

'I was wrong, Captain,' Banks said.

'What do you mean?'

'Chalipun is still here.'

'What?' Peters blurted out.

'I said that the wily son of a bitch is still here. See?'

Peters paled as every slab of granite around Chiricahua Springs suddenly seemed to sprout an Apache.

Banks spit in the dust at his feet. 'Saracen was right.'

All 'B' troop stopped what they were doing and stared at the Indians. A few muttered curses could be heard as the stark reality of their situation set in. The thirty had grown. Now there seemed to be more like fifty.

Peters' face started to show the first signs of panic, and Banks knew enough about new officers to know that this one was about to crack.

'Easy, Captain. If they wanted to kill us, they'd have started shooting by now. Maybe he wants to talk.'

Peters' eyes darted left and right. He took a tentative step back, dropping his hand to his holstered sidearm. He fumbled at the flap with trembling fingers.

'Easy, Captain,' Banks warned him again.

'You let him pull that gun and we're all dead, Tyrell,' a seasoned trooper called out.

Banks took a step towards the officer, his hand held out. 'Leave it be, Captain.'

But the man was beyond reason. He was in the grip of such fear that his only instinct was survival. And to survive, Peters could only think of one way.

He pulled his gun.

There was nothing Banks could do. 'Shit!'

The Apaches opened up with deadly effect. They had rifles, they had cover, and above all else, they had the high ground.

Chiricahua Springs rocked with the sound of gunfire. Banks grabbed for his rifle and worked its lever. A loud slap caught his attention and he noticed the red blotch on the front of Peters' uniform where a slug had slammed into the captain's chest. The officer's six-gun fell from his lifeless fingers and he slumped to the ground.

All around Banks, angry lead hornets snapped through the desert air. Small geysers of dirt exploded from the ground as bullets ploughed into it. Screams from troopers split the afternoon.

The old scout dived behind a chunk of granite no bigger than a pig. Two other troopers joined him there as they desperately tried to find cover.

'Damn it, Tyrell, I told you to stop him.'

It dawned on Banks that this was the trooper who'd shouted the warning. 'He was beyond listening, son.'

Banks rose and fired a shot from his rifle at a puff of gunsmoke further up the ridge. He levered and fired again. A grim satisfaction settled over him as he started to fight back. He fired three more shots before dropping back behind cover.

A grunt from beside Banks drew his attention. He looked at the trooper closest to him and saw the man start to slump forward, still clutching his carbine. The trooper wouldn't be needing it any time soon, as a bullet had struck him in the chest just above his heart.

Banks looked back behind himself and saw the carnage where 'B' company had been caught out in the open, blue-clad bodies strewn everywhere. In such a short period of time, Banks figured they'd lost fifteen men.

He saw a wounded trooper trying to drag himself towards the cover of some brush. Bullets splashed grit all around him as the Apache tried to kill him. One of the man's friends broke from behind a rock to help him. On reaching the fallen trooper, he grabbed him by the collar and began to drag him across the rough ground towards the brush he so desperately needed to reach.

The old scout saw a bullet strike the rescuer in the chest. The blue material of the man's shirt seemed to flutter as a puff of dust exploded from it. The trooper released his grip on his friend and staggered back a couple of steps.

He gathered himself and reached out for the collar once more, only to be stopped when another slug burned deep into his guts. The man sank to his knees, clutching at the wound. A third shot punched into his brain and he flopped back on to the ground.

More slugs burned through the air around Banks, forcing him to shrink lower. Now, soldiers were dying with regular monotony until there were no more left to kill.

Only Banks remained, out of ammunition and cowering behind the same rock.

A long shadow fell over him and the old scout looked up. Before him stood a tall, muscular figure with long, dark hair, his face the colour of copper, his eyes dark and brooding.

'You are the only one left, white-eye,' Chalipun grunted.

Banks swallowed and prepared himself to meet his maker. He stood up and fixed his gaze on the Apache chief's eyes. 'You aim to kill me too?'

Chalipun stared at him for an inordinately long time then shook his head. 'I let you live. You tell them of the great victory Chalipun have here.'

Banks felt a flood of relief wash over him. He looked at the Apache and hesitated before asking, 'The children?'

*

Saracen climbed on to the back of his horse and stared at O'Rourke. 'Come on, Mike. We'd best go take a look.'

O'Rourke nodded. 'I guess so.' Turning to the other troopers, he called out, 'Mount up, men!'

It had been at least an hour since the gunfire had abated and not one Indian had passed them by, which to Saracen's thinking, meant that maybe Peters had bested them and had the survivors restrained.

O'Rourke eased his mount in beside the scout's as they rode along and said, 'What are you thinking?'

Saracen shrugged. 'Maybe I was wrong. Maybe it wasn't a trap.'

'If it was,' suggested the sergeant, 'you'd think that the Apache would have come south, either way.'

'That's the bit I can't figure. If Peters caught them by surprise, then yes, why didn't anyone try to skedaddle out our way? And if it was a trap, then you'd think Chalipun would want to get across the border as fast as possible and leave it behind him before any more troops arrive. I don't know. Maybe I'm overthinking it.'

O'Rourke suddenly pulled his horse up. 'I guess we'll find out.'

Saracen reined in his own mount and followed the sergeant's gaze. The sky up ahead was dotted with large black shapes lazily spiralling towards the ground.

'About time you fellers showed,' Banks growled, emerging from behind a large boulder.

Saracen focused on the scout. 'What happened? Where's the captain?'

Banks' face fell. 'You were right. They were waiting for us. We got ourselves surrounded. I'm the only one who's left. And that's because Chalipun let me live.'

Saracen heard O'Rourke curse.

'Was there any sign of the children?'

Banks held up a finger. Then he walked around to the rear of the rock and reappeared with the children in tow. 'He left them with me.'

'Where did they go?'

'They rode out the way we came in.'

Saracen looked about him at the men who were left. Then he stared at the children. He turned in the saddle and said to O'Rourke, 'Let's get back to the fort while we can. Then I can quit.'

'You what!'

'You heard me, Colonel. I said I'm done.'

Colonel Walt Mercer rose from his seat and ran a thorny hand through his whitening hair. 'Damn it, Saracen, I need you now more than ever. With Chalipun still out there, and me down roughly forty men now, I need you to scout.'

'You've still got Tyrell.'

'I don't want him. I want you!' he thundered and walked across the office to the map pinned on the wall. He drew a broad circle on it. 'You're the only one who knows the territory inside out.'

Saracen shook his head. 'I'm done with scouting, Colonel. Plain and simple.'

Mercer could see that there was no changing the scout's mind. He shook his head. 'I'll be sorry to see you go, Blaine. What are you going to do?'

'I'm going to get as far away from the army as possible. Might go back to Texas and visit my family.'

Mercer moved forwards and stuck out his right hand. 'Good luck, Saracen. We'll miss you around here.'

Largo, Texas
When Saracen laid eyes on the ranch house he knew something was wrong. There was no woodsmoke coming from the old stone chimney, no movement in the ranch yard, no animals in the corral.

When he got closer he could see that the ranch looked run down, and he noticed two graves under the tree beside the barn.

Saracen dismounted and walked slowly towards them. A knot began to form deep in the pit of his stomach. He figured the graves to be no more than two months old. The wooden markers were faced away from him and he hesitated momentarily before stepping around them to see.

It was like a punch to Saracen's guts when he saw the names:

Bill Saracen
Died 1879
Elizabeth Saracen
Died 1879

21

They were dead. His parents; both of them. The pain of it created an immediate physical ache in his chest. Then all at once he thought of his sister: where was Victoria?

Saracen turned away from the graves and walked across to the house. He climbed the steps on to the verandah and opened the screen door, which voiced its protest. Then he tried the timber door, turning the handle, and it swung freely, so he walked inside.

The interior was a mess. As though things had been rifled through. In the kitchen, there were plates on the table with rotten food. All the furniture, whether upturned or not, was covered in dust.

What the hell had happened? He walked over to his parents' room and opened the door. Even the side cupboard built for his mother by his father's own hands had been upturned.

He needed to find someone who'd tell him what happened. He needed to go into town.

In the years he'd been gone, Largo hadn't changed much. Even in the last rays of the late afternoon. Gotten a little bigger, maybe, even had a new court-house, but other than that, it was pretty much the same. Even most of the people.

He tied his horse to the hitch rail outside the jail and went inside. The man at the desk was a little greyer and a little broader than the last time Saracen had seen him, but he was still the same Lem Bates.

'Howdy, Lem,' Saracen greeted him.

The man looked up from his paper and stared hard at the newcomer. He frowned, thought a little, and then recognition dawned.

'By gosh darn, it is you!' he exclaimed. 'Blaine Saracen, as I live and breathe.'

'Yeah, it's me.'

Bates came from his chair and shook hands with the newcomer. 'Damn, boy, it's good to see you. The last I heard, you was scouting for the cavalry against the Apache out in Arizona.'

'Yeah, I was.'

The expression on the man's lined face changed. 'Did you get my letter, boy?'

'No.'

'Hell. I sent it a couple of months back. It was about ... about. . . .'

'I know, Lem. I was out at the ranch.'

'I'm sure sorry, Blaine,' Bates said with a shake of his head. He walked across to the front window of his office and looked out at the street.

'What happened, Lem?' Saracen asked.

Bates turned and stared at him. 'You ever hear of a feller named Black Ted Allen?'

'Yeah.'

'Him and his gang came through here. Robbed the bank. Killed Old Cyrus Ryan, the bank manager. On the way out they shot my deputy.

You remember young Cecil Tailor?'

Saracen nodded.

'They just shot him down in the street on their way out of town. Wounded a couple of others, too.'

'My parents, Lem.'

The sheriff's gaze dropped for a moment and then

he brought it back up. 'Your pa and ma's place happened to be on the route they chose to ride. They stopped there long enough to steal food and horses. Your pa must have tried to stop them. They killed them both.'

It was a hard thing to hear and Saracen could only imagine what their last moments had been like.

'What about Victoria? What happened to her, Lem?'

Now the sheriff's expression grew into one of pain. 'I don't know. We tried to find her but couldn't. She. . . .'

Saracen exploded. 'They took her!'

'Yes.'

'What are you doing about it? Why didn't you go after them?'

'I did, Blaine, honest I did. But the posse lost them after three days. The trail just vanished. We spent a further three days trying to find it again, but we had no luck. I even sent wires out to surrounding counties, but they came up empty. They just disappeared.'

Saracen remained silent.

'We really tried, Blaine.'

'Not hard enough,' Saracen snapped and whirled about.

'Where are you going?'

'To find Victoria.'

'What about the ranch? It's yours now.'

Saracen ignored him and kept walking. He'd never given a damn about the ranch before. Why start now?

CHAPTER 2

Crescent Creek, Texas, 1880

Deputy United States Marshal Dan Bliss drew rein outside Crescent Creek, some ten miles west of Wichita Falls, and waited. The hot Texas sun shone down over his right shoulder as it started its steady descent towards the distant horizon. The middle-aged, broad-shouldered lawman out of Fort Smith stared at the town in silence.

Somewhere in the town was Flash Jack Baron, owner of the Texas Rose Saloon and supplier of illegal whiskey into the Nations. Which was why Bliss was there.

Baron had been feeding the Creeks and the Cherokee enough rotgut whiskey to keep them drunk for weeks. And at that point in time, alcohol was the last thing they needed. The mixed-blood Cherokees and the black Creeks were locking horns over an invisible line called a border. The Cherokee riders targeted the Creek Lighthorsemen, who were the local police, and the Creeks were riding into Cherokee lands and starting to shoot up their homes. It had to stop, so Judge Isaac Parker had sent Bliss to find Baron, and in his own words, to 'put the bastard out of business before the Nations are torn apart!'

There was a noise behind Bliss and he turned in the saddle. The Tumbleweed wagon rattled to a stop, atop its seat a baldheaded man wearing a top hat. Amos Faraday on this trip was Bliss' deputy and cook. A tough law officer in his own right, Faraday had volunteered to help his friend apprehend Baron and bring him in.

'About time you caught up,' Bliss growled. 'You been sleeping?'

'Can't help it if you picked out the slowest horses in the dang corral.'

Bliss grunted.

Faraday leaned down and grabbed up a sawn-off messenger gun, broke it open, and checked the loads. They were the same as the other six times he'd checked them.

'Did you think they might have ridden off somewhere?' Bliss asked.

Faraday stared at him. 'Never can be too sure. Did I tell you what happened to me that time I rode into Tahlequah after the Eagle-Claw brothers?'

Bliss rolled his eyes. 'Only every other day.'

'Yeah? Well, you know what happened, don't you?'

Faraday had ridden into Tahlequah twelve months before, chasing Jack and Johnny Eagle-Claw. The night before he entered the town he'd set to cleaning his messenger gun, as he often did before turning in.

However, this time he forgot to reload it.

'So, there I was—'

Bliss rolled his eyes again and eased his mount forwards. Behind him, Faraday's voice started to fade, then the noise of the tumbleweed wagon rattled again as it began to move. Bliss hadn't wanted the jail on wheels, but Faraday had insisted.

'You never can tell,' he said.

Bliss shook his head and mumbled. 'Yeah. You never can tell.'

Crescent Creek wasn't a big town, but it was busy. It consisted of the main street, three side streets, and a central crossroads, upon which was the largest saloon in town, the Texas Rose.

As Isaac Parker's lawmen made their way along the main street, people stopped and stared. It wasn't the first time a federal marshal had arrived in Crescent Creek, nor was it the first time they'd seen a tumbleweed wagon. It just didn't happen that often.

False-fronted storefronts were commonplace on either side, while the few trees left inside the town limits weren't. The boardwalks were lined with townsfolk. Every one of them stopped what they were doing to watch.

'Anybody would think they ain't never seen a lawman before,' Faraday grumbled.

'Maybe they have, and they're waiting to see what happens next.'

'Sheriff's office is up there on the left,' the wagon driver pointed out.

They drew to a halt outside the jail and climbed down. Stomping their way up the steps on to the boardwalk, they pushed in through the door.

Sheriff Bart Fordice was sitting behind his desk, enjoying his coffee when he looked up and saw them enter. His face changed from one of satisfaction to one of annoyance. The large, middle-aged man with long sideburns thumped his cup down on to the top of the scarred desktop and slopped its contents.

'What the hell do you want, Bliss?' he growled.

Bliss smiled. 'Well, well. Did they finally run you out of Kansas, Fordice?'

Faraday said, 'I take it you two know each other?'

'Yeah. Up in Kansas. He wasn't wearing a badge then. In actual fact, he was on the other side of the law. Accused of holding up a stage.'

'The charges weren't proved,' Fordice blurted out.

Bliss nodded. 'That's right. Still don't mean you didn't do it, though.'

'Don't mean I did,' he grouched again. 'Why are you here?'

'Baron.'

A mirthless smile split Fordice's face. 'This I got to see. You intend on taking him in?'

'That's right. Judge Parker wants him taken in.'

'Parker ain't got no jurisdiction down here this side of the Red.'

'I have, though, and Baron has been selling liquor in the Nations. Judge wants it stopped.'

'Well, good luck, Bliss. Hope you get your head blowed off.'

'Faraday, lock him up,' Bliss ordered.

'The hell you say,' Fordice cursed. His hand dropped to his holstered six-gun. 'You ain't locking me in my own jail.'

'I'll give you a choice. You get in that cell or I'll bury you. I ain't having you walking around where you can shoot me in the back.'

The small room was filled with the ratcheting of the twin hammers going back on Faraday's messenger gun. 'And if he don't kill you, I will. Start walking.'

'Piss on you, Bliss,' Fordice snarled.

Bliss smiled. 'I wouldn't let you even if I was on fire.'

The doors to the jail clanged shut and drowned out the savage curses Fordice still hurled at both men. Faraday turned back to Bliss and asked, 'What now?'

'We go do our job.'

Flash Jack Baron leaned back on the fancy daybed he'd had shipped from Chicago while a whore named Mary snuggled up to him. The door crashed open, disturbing them both.

'By Christ, Lefty, this better be good, or else,' Baron fumed.

Lefty Wainright stared at Mary while she straightened her clothing.

'Lefty?' Baron growled.

The gunman's eyes flickered back to his boss. 'Hmm?'

'You came in here for a reason. What the hell was it?'

Lefty waved the stump of his left arm in the air, the reason for his name. 'A couple of marshals just rode into town with a tumbleweed wagon.'

Baron pressed his lips together, the effect making his pencil-thin moustache even thinner. 'Who's in it?'

'No one. It's empty.'

Baron came off the daybed and unfurled himself to his full height of six-one. He straightened his suit pants, put on his shirt and coat over his wide torso, then tucked a small pocket pistol into his waistband.

He walked across the room to where Mary stood next to his hardwood desk and took out ten dollars. He put it inside the top of her bodice between her breasts. He looked into her blue eyes as he gave one a gentle squeeze and said, 'Don't go too far.'

She smiled and said in her southern drawl, 'I'll be right here waiting, sugar.'

The two men walked out and into the main barroom. It was busy, as always, for Baron had the best liquor, the best girls and the best gambling tables. He'd spent a lot of money on the Texas Rose: chandeliers, wood panelling, hardwood bar, brass fittings and footrail. It didn't come cheap.

Then there were the girls. All top class from back east. All clean and inspected by the town doctor once a month to make sure they remained that way. But it cost money, and there was only one way to get the steady supply of cash he required to do it. Baron sold whiskey to the Indians in the Nations.

As he strolled through the room he was greeted by many of the customers, for in Crescent Creek, Baron was about the most popular man around. And the deadliest.

A loud curse was followed by a high-pitched scream over in the far right corner of the room near the foot of the stairs. Two men suddenly came erect out of their seats and the table where they were seated was turned upside down. A red-headed whore lurched back with a hand over her mouth as the two started to trade blows with each other.

A quick glance around the room from Baron located one of his four guards, who was about to address the problem. He watched as the big bearded man wielded the sawn-off shotgun in his hands with practised skill. When he was done, both the protagonists were down and motionless.

Moments later they'd been dragged from the saloon and dumped out on the street.

It wasn't long after that the batwings opened and Faraday, in company with Dan Bliss, pushed through and stood just inside.

Their eyes searched the room until they locked gazes with Baron. Bliss took a step forward and said in a loud voice, 'Jack Baron, we're here to take you in!'

The smile on Baron's face said it all. His voice was cold and emotionless. 'Come ahead and try.'

Saracen couldn't remember the whore's name, and he didn't much care either. He'd come here to ask questions. None of which were answered.

He'd ridden into Crescent Creek not long after midday. He found himself a room, a meal, and now the company of, in his opinion, a fine woman. However, the whore might not have thought the same of him, especially after he threw her bodily on to the bed beside him when the gunfire downstairs erupted.

'Hey! What the hell are you doing?' she cried out. 'We was just getting to the good part.'

Saracen cursed under his breath and rolled off the steel-framed bed and pulled on his pants and boots. He didn't worry about the shirt, he'd come back for that. Then, before he exited the room, he tucked the .45 Schofield into his pants and picked up the Winchester.

As he strode along the hall with powerful strides, the gunfire seemed to go up a notch. Doors opened, and heads appeared.

By the time Saracen reached the landing, most of the customers below had cleared out or dived behind overturned tables. He levered a round into the Winchester's breech and peered over the balustrade. Down below he could see that two men had been shot and another five were doing all they could to kill a single man who found himself behind the hardwood bar.

One of the fallen moved. It was only slight, but it was enough to catch Saracen's attention. And then he saw the shiny object on the fallen man's shirt. He was a lawman.

But Saracen wasn't the only one who'd seen the lawman move. So too had the one-handed man, who at that moment was sighting along the barrel of his Colt ready to snuff out the downed lawman's life.

'Not today, asshole,' Saracen growled and brought the Winchester to his shoulder. Once the foresight had settled on the killer, he fired.

The rifle bucked and slammed back into his shoulder. The .45-.70 slug erupted from the barrel and flew true, slamming into the side of the one-handed man's head and blowing his brains over the upturned chair next to him in a bloody spray. He collapsed to the floor and didn't move.

A cry of anger rang out through the crash of gunfire, and Saracen saw another one of the shooters look up in his direction, and start to swing up the six-gun in his fist. He never made it.

Saracen levered once more, and the Winchester roared. The bullet slammed into the man, driving him back with a sudden violence. Saracen worked the action again and shot the man in the chest.

The three killers who were left turned their gazes to the landing and the man who'd joined the fight. They raised their guns in his direction and cut loose with a wild fusillade. Saracen ducked back and the bullets from below hammered into the ceiling above him.

With their attention turned to their new adversary, the man behind the bar had the opportunity he needed to strike back. He came up with a six-gun in his fist and fired at a big man with a sawn-off shotgun. The man cried out, dropped the weapon, and collapsed.

Now the men, the killers, were caught in what was mostly a crossfire. There was only one thing they could do: they threw down their guns and put their hands in the air.

Then came eerie silence, punctuated by the moan

of a wounded man.

Saracen covered the room with his Winchester and called down, 'Are you all right, friend?'

The man behind the bar came to his feet, his boots crunching on the broken glass beneath his feet. He stared up at his shirtless saviour. 'I'm fine, thank you kindly. Who might you be?'

Saracen started down the stairs. 'The name's Blaine Saracen. You?'

'Deputy United States marshal, Dan Bliss.'

Saracen reached the bottom of the stairs and said, 'Bit of a spot you got yourself into.'

Bliss saw Faraday down, and cursed. He hurried to the deputy's side and looked over his wound while Saracen kept the two remaining men covered. Both he recognized. One was a guard, the other was the owner, Baron.

The saloon owner growled, 'I'll give you five hundred to put a bullet in that son of a bitch.'

Bliss raised his head and picked out a bystander from the crowd that had started to gather. 'Get a damned doctor in here.'

'Go on, do it,' Baron snapped. 'Five hundred to kill him now.'

Bliss glared at the saloon owner.

Saracen eyed him and asked, 'You got that on you?'

Baron nodded. 'In my pocket.'

The scout glanced at Bliss and then back at Baron. He stepped in closer to the saloon owner. 'Which one?'

'Inside my coat.'

Saracen reached inside and took out the money. He held it up and turned to Bliss. 'You want some of this?'

Bliss shook his head. 'You keep it. He won't need it where he's going.'

'Son of a bitch,' Baron cursed and lunged at Saracen.

The scout stopped him short with a quick jab from the barrel of the Winchester. Air rushed from the man's lungs as he doubled over, and Saracen said, 'I'm not some hired gun you can buy with your money, Baron. However, I'll take it all the same. You should be careful which man's gun you try to purchase.'

The scout glanced at Bliss. 'You want me to put these fellers somewhere?'

'It would help if you took them over to the jail,' Bliss allowed. 'You'll find the sheriff there occupying one of his own cells too. Get him out.'

Saracen nodded. 'I'll take care of it.'

'Get the hell away from him, you drunk fool!' Bliss snarled and pushed the intoxicated medico away from Faraday.

Saracen had just entered after locking up the prisoners. He frowned and said, 'You got a problem?'

Bliss stabbed a finger at the disheveled doctor. 'The bastard is drunk. He's useless.'

'Can you do it?' Saracen asked.

Bliss held up a hand. 'These ain't made for getting bullets out, Saracen.'

A stern expression came over the scout's face. 'I guess I'll have to do it, then. Get him up on the bar where he's a bit higher.'

They lifted Faraday from the floor and he moaned as the pain ripped through him. Once he was on the bar top, Saracen tore the shirt completely open and stared at the livid-looking hole an inch or so below Faraday's heart. It still pulsed bright red blood.

'You . . . you shouldn't do . . . do thish,' the doctor protested thickly.

Saracen glared at him then said, 'Give me your bag, Doc.'

The man gave him an indignant look and tucked it under his arm. He said, 'I'll do . . . no sush . . . thing. Theesh are fine . . . inst . . . instrumensh.'

Bliss cursed under his breath and ripped the bag free. He placed it on the bar where Saracen could reach it.

'Hey! You. . . !'

'Shut the hell up!' Bliss barked.

Saracen opened the bag and found something that looked like scissors, except they had flat edges on them for grasping things. The scout looked up at the doctor. 'Are these for getting bullets out?'

The doctor nodded.

Then Saracen found a scalpel and put it with the forceps.

There was a loud clunk as Bliss placed a bottle of whiskey on the counter. 'Here.'

The scout popped the cork and splashed the fiery liquid over the blade as well as the wound. He then said to Bliss, 'You'd best hold on to him while I make this hole bigger so I can get them other things that are in there.'

The marshal held Faraday while Saracen opened the wound for the bullet extractors.

'At least you won't get blood on your shirt,' Bliss pointed out.

Saracen realized he was still shirtless, and as he worked, the rock-hard muscles of his chest rippled.

He splashed more whiskey, this time on the extractors. He looked around and saw a scantily dressed, black-haired whore watching. 'You, get over here and help the marshal.'

Her eyebrows shot up. 'Me?'

'Yes, damn it.'

She hurried across and stood beside them.

'Hold him still.'

No sooner had she taken a hold than Saracen pushed the extractors into the wound. With a gasp and then a roar, Faraday came to life and tried to rise to rid himself of the burning pain. The veins in his neck and face bulged as he writhed violently. Saracen had to stop.

'Hold him still, damn it,' he cursed.

'If you ain't noticed, we're trying,' Bliss snapped.

'Christ,' the scout muttered and with a clenched fist, clipped the wounded marshal under the jaw, putting a stop to his movements altogether.

Bliss nodded in satisfaction. 'That'll work.'

'Then let's get this damned thing out before he wakes up,' Saracen growled.

Two hours later the sun was down, and the two men sat

at a table in the empty saloon. Faraday was resting comfortably in a room upstairs while the whore who'd helped them watched over him. Saracen was now fully clothed after he'd gone back to his room to get his shirt. Between the two sat a half-empty bottle of whiskey and two partially filled glasses. Both men looked tired.

'Tell me, Saracen, what is it you do?' Bliss asked as he sipped his drink.

Saracen sighed. 'At the moment I'm doing something personal. I was scouting over Arizona way.'

'Had enough?'

'Enough of damned fools.'

'You ever thought about pinning on a badge?'

Saracen tossed his drink back and felt the burn as it slid down his throat. He shook his head. 'Not me.'

'The work's regular. Pay's not much, but Judge Parker is always looking for good men.'

Again, Saracen shook his head. 'I'll pass. Like I said, I've got something else on.'

Bliss shrugged. 'Pity. Mind if I ask what?'

'Looking for my sister. She's with an outlaw bunch led by Black Ted Allen.'

'That's bad company right there, Saracen.'

He nodded. 'The son-of-a-bitch killed my parents and took her along with him and his gang.'

'What did the law do about it?'

'Nothing. The sheriff took out a posse but found nothing.'

'How long you been looking?'

'Bit over six months. But they seem to have gone to ground.'

'Could I offer you temporary employment then? I need to get these fellers back to Arkansas, and Faraday ain't in much shape to help out. I'll deputize you until we get back. After that you can go your own way. Maybe they've heard something in Fort Smith.'

The scout thought hard about the offer.

'I'll pay you twenty dollars,' Bliss said, trying to sweeten the pot.

Saracen nodded. 'All right, I'll help out. But after it's done, I'm gone.'

Bliss smiled and picked up the whiskey bottle. 'Well, shoot. That deserves another go around.'

CHAPTER 3

Anson's Post, Choctaw Nation

Anson's Post was named after the trader who'd set up on the small stream in the fifties before the war. Now it was a small town, with the old trading post serving as the jail for the Choctaw Lighthorse.

The tumbleweed wagon rattled along the rutted track which passed for the main street. The steel-rimmed wheels lurched into a water-filled hole, spraying the water outwards, adding to the muddy mess left over from the previous night's rain.

Faraday sat on the driver's seat beside Bliss, a blanket wrapped around him, his face a pasty grey colour. Saracen rode along behind them, the star pinned to his shirt glinting in the sunlight.

Bliss drew the wagon to a halt outside the old trading post, and an Indian came out and stood under the awning. His long black hair flowed from beneath what had once been a light grey hat, now a dirty and sweat-stained impression of its former self.

He looked up at Bliss. 'Hello, Dan Bliss.'

'Hello, Henry Grey Elk. How's the Lighthorse business?'

'Quiet,' the Choctaw said with an abrupt nod. 'I see you are busy.'

'Yeah. Taking a couple prisoners back to Fort Smith.' His face grew grim. 'Hopefully to hang.'

Henry moved out further to get a look at the prisoners. He grunted when his dark eyes settled on one in particular. 'I see you have Baron in your cage. It is a good day. In fact, I have some of his whiskey inside that myself and Jim Tall Eagle took from some Creeks who got it over in Chickasaw territory.'

'Well, he won't be doing it anymore,' Bliss said. Then he asked, 'Is your wife around at all? Faraday here stopped a slug, enacting our duty. He could use some nursing overnight.'

Henry nodded. 'Little Bird will take care of him. Who is your other deputy?'

'That's Blaine Saracen. He helped us out when the bullets were flying,' Bliss turned in the seat. 'Saracen, come up here.'

Saracen eased his horse forward. 'What's up?'

'Nothing. I wanted you to meet Henry Grey Elk. He's head of the local Choctaw Lighthorse. Henry, Blaine Saracen.'

Henry came out and held up a hand. Saracen took it and shook. 'Pleased to meet you, Henry.'

Henry nodded and stepped back.

Bliss smiled. 'I hope you've got an appetite, Saracen. Henry's wife is a mighty fine cook. I swear she could take buffalo chips and turn them into a feast.'

The Lighthorseman gave Saracen a wry smile and said, 'Let's hope we never have to find out.'

Their chuckles were interrupted by Faraday who'd been silent until now. 'You fellers forgot about me or something? Howdy, Henry.'

'Hello, Amos.'

'I heard someone mention food,' Faraday grumbled.

Bliss chuckled. 'I swear, Amos. You'd be dead and buried and still looking for something to eat.'

All of them laughed, and then Bliss's expression changed. 'You ain't heard of Black Ted Allen haunting these parts of late?'

Saracen tensed.

Henry shook his head. 'I ain't heard of him since he was raising hell down in Texas.'

'If you happen to, can you let me know?'

'Sure.'

'Hey,' said Faraday. 'What about the food?'

'Are you sure there's only a few of them?' Willy Pete asked the scar-faced Creek. 'We ain't going to get into town and get all shot to hell by more of them?'

Scar-faced Sam Moonlight glared at the man next to him and growled, 'Shut the hell up, Willy, or I'll shoot you myself.'

Willy Pete's horse shifted under him. 'I was only making sure, Sam.'

'Just shut up.'

There were six of them, all Creek Indians, come to Anson's Post to get the whiskey that was taken from

42

them. There was no way that they were going to let the damned Choctaw lawmen get away with it.

'If you get half a chance,' Sam Moonlight continued, 'kill the two Lighthorsemen. Shoot them dead.'

They all knew he meant it. They'd seen him kill before. For no apparent reason other than just because he could.

'Come on,' he snapped. 'Let's do this.'

'Looks like you got trouble coming this way,' Saracen said as he looked out the window of the jail at the six horsemen riding along the street. All had rifles in their hands, which meant trouble.

Henry walked across to the window and looked for himself. He muttered something under his breath, and then said, 'That is all we need.'

'You know them?'

Henry nodded. 'Yes. The one out front is Scar-faced Sam Moonlight. He's not a nice Indian.'

Bliss hurried across to stand beside them. 'What the hell does that ornery son of a bitch want?'

'The whiskey,' Henry stated.

'Sure looks like he means to have it,' Saracen pointed out.

'It does.'

Bliss said, 'You figure he'll ride off if we go out there and tell him he can't have it?'

Henry shook his head. 'No.'

'You mean we're going to have to shoot him?'

'The man's a killer. They only understand one thing.'

43

Saracen checked the loads in his Schofield. 'I guess we'd better go out there and say hello.'

Bliss nodded. 'Coming, Henry?'

The Choctaw Lighthorseman walked across to a gun rack on the wall and took down a sawn-off shotgun. He turned back to face Bliss and Saracen. 'I ain't got nothing better to do.'

'Well, it's your territory, your show,' Bliss pointed out.

Henry led them out through the door. He stepped down on to the street and stood with his hand resting on the butt of his Colt. He was by no means fast with a gun, but what he lacked in speed, the Choctaw made up for with accuracy.

The six Creeks dismounted and walked towards the three of them. They stopped with around twenty feet between them, the scar-faced leader's hand hovering over the butt of his gun.

Saracen's right hand grasped the Schofield on his left hip, ready to bring it into action. Bliss stood with a Winchester in his hands, hammer back, finger on the trigger.

'What do you want in Choctaw territory, Moonlight?' Henry asked. 'If it is the whiskey you've come for, you might as well turn and ride back out.'

'Are you saying it ain't here?' Sam Moonlight asked.

'It's here.'

'Then how about you give us back what's ours?'

'And how about I give you an ounce of lead for your troubles,' Bliss stated.

'Who are you, white man?' Sam snapped.

44

Bliss drew back the lapel on his coat to reveal the badge. 'I'm Deputy United States Marshal Dan Bliss. The gent over there is Deputy Blaine Saracen.'

A troubled expression washed over the scarred face of the Creek, and then he pushed it aside. A problem he hadn't allowed for.

'This has nothing to do with you. Stand aside.'

Not the first shootout Saracen had been in, he was quite proficient with the Schofield, and some would say, fast. He waited patiently to see how it would play out. With a little luck, they would go away.

Bliss said, 'Can't do that.'

'Then you'll die right along with this Choctaw asshole.'

With that, Moonlight started to draw his six-gun.

It was the Schofield which fired first. The .45 calibre slug slammed into the Creek's chest a fraction of a heartbeat before Bliss's. Henry's first shot crashed into Willy Pete and knocked him back. The Creek fought to keep his feet, but a second slug ripped through his throat in a bright spray of blood. He dropped to the ground and flopped around like a fish out of water.

Saracen's second shot knocked a tall Creek from his feet, while Bliss's burned deep into the guts of a shorter man, doubling him over.

The two Creeks who were left upright, fired with wild abandon. The bullets sprayed through the air as fear overcame them, especially after witnessing the deaths of their friends. Saracen felt one tug at his sleeve as it passed through it, the heat warming his skin.

He heard Bliss grunt as a bullet hammered home in his chest, and the marshal buckled at the knees, a red blotch high up on the front of his shirt.

Henry's next shot nailed one of the last two Creeks flush in the face. The slug burrowed into the man's brain by way of the bridge of his nose. The would-be killer crumpled into an untidy heap, the six-gun he had used falling beside him.

Saracen's second last shot put an end to the final shooter. The bullet hammered into his chest and tore through vital organs. The Creek cried out with pain and fell. For a few heartbeats, he gasped for air, and then died.

Saracen broke the Schofield open and dropped the spent rounds on to the ground before replacing them with fresh loads. A groan brought his attention to the wounded Bliss. He hurried across to him while Henry checked the Creeks.

Bliss was hit hard and his face was a pasty grey colour from the pain, which burned deep in his body.

'Bastard got me good,' he hissed through clenched teeth.

'Let's have a look at you,' Saracen said, opening the wounded marshal's shirt. He placed a hand firmly over the bleeding hole. 'I reckon we'd best get someone to look at that.'

'I ain't too sure if I'm going to make it through this one.'

Saracen glanced about at the crowd as it started to gather. He sought out Henry and called across to him. 'Henry, do you have a doctor in town?'

The Choctaw policeman turned and shook his head. 'My wife usually does all of the doctoring around here when it needs doing.'

'You'd best get her or Bliss ain't going to make it.'

Saracen looked down at the semi-conscious lawman. 'Hold on, Dan. We'll get that slug out of you, and you'll be fine.'

Bliss looked at him through half-open eyes for a moment, and then closed them. Blood ran between Saracen's fingers as the wound showed no sign of the blood flow slowing.

Again, Saracen said, 'Just hold on.'

A few minutes later a slim, not unattractive woman with long, raven-coloured hair appeared through the gathered crowd. She glanced at Saracen as she knelt beside Bliss.

'I am Nita,' she said as she removed Saracen's bloody hands from the wound. 'I am Henry's wife.'

'I'm Saracen.'

She raised her head and stared at him. 'We need to get him inside.'

With the help of four others plus Henry, they raised Bliss from the ground and carried him to Henry's house where Nita could take care of him. Then all Saracen could do was wait and see if he'd pull through.

Saracen was seated on the veranda of the Grey Elk home, waiting for news about Bliss. It had been a couple of hours at least since the shootout, and the sun was a low orange ball in the western sky, starting to slip below the horizon, fingers of colour reaching out as though trying to cling to the day.

There was a noise beside him and he glanced about. Faraday moved slowly and sat on a chair beside him.

'What are you doing out here?' Saracen asked him.

'Me? I'm fine. I was wondering about Bliss. Any news?'

'Nope.'

Faraday scratched his bald head. 'I hope he'll be OK. Me and him has ridden many trails together. He's a good man. Did I ever tell you about the time me and Bliss was chasing the Stone gang?'

Saracen shook his head. He guessed it was Faraday's way of trying to block out the worry about his friend. 'Nope.'

'Well, we was trailing the Stone gang who'd slipped into the Nations after they robbed a bank in Arkansas. They killed two marshals and a couple of Indian police and disappeared. Just vanished like a wisp of smoke. So, me and Bliss rode into this small settlement called Jacob's Well. Seemed right peaceful, until all of a sudden like, we was getting shot at. Seems we stumbled on Stone and his gang.'

The door opened and Henry stepped outside. Saracen stood and stared at the Choctaw policeman. 'How is he?'

'He wants to see you both.'

Saracen shifted his gaze to Faraday and then back. He nodded. 'OK.'

The pair followed Henry inside and he showed

them through to a dimly lit room. Inside was Henry's wife, Nita. She smiled at them and said, 'He will be fine if I can keep him in bed long enough.'

Nita's gaze locked with the scout's, and for a moment he stared at her in the orange glow before he looked to Bliss.

Nita said, 'I'll leave you to it.'

The door snicked shut and the pair stood beside the bed, staring down at the pasty-faced Bliss.

'So what is it that couldn't wait until morning?' Faraday asked.

'Are you right to ride, Amos?' Bliss asked in a weak voice.

'I can sit a wagon,' Faraday said.

'Good. You and Saracen take our prisoners back to Fort Smith. Get them in the judge's jail. Saracen's in charge.'

Saracen opened his mouth to protest, but Bliss cut him off. 'Don't say anything. You are the only fit one out of us all. Faraday ain't fit so you'll have the extra responsibility. You have a problem with that, Amos?'

'Nope. I'll take my orders from Saracen.'

'Right. Just get them back. If they give you any trouble, shoot them. I'll be back when I'm able.'

Saracen nodded. 'OK, Dan. But just until we get back.'

'Good, you leave first thing in the morning.'

Saracen said, 'Come on, Amos, let's get out of here so he can get some rest.'

'You go ahead,' Bliss said. 'I want to talk to Amos for a moment. He'll be along directly.'

Saracen shrugged and walked out, closing the door. In the living room he found Nita. Again he found himself staring at her appearance in the orange lamplight.

'Is he OK?' she asked.

'Yeah. Ah, we're pulling out in the morning.'

He saw alarm come to her eyes. He hurriedly added, 'Amos and me. Not Bliss. We're taking the prisoners back to Fort Smith.'

Relief flooded Nita's face, and she said, 'I'll get some supplies together for you both.'

'There's no need for that, ma'am. We've got plenty of grub.'

'Well, I'll give you extra.'

'That'd be right kind of you, ma'am.'

'Call me Nita,' she insisted.

'Only if you call me Blaine.'

'OK, Blaine.'

'Can I ask you a question, ma'am? Without being too personal.'

She smiled. 'How about I be the judge of that? Ask away.'

Saracen hesitated a moment and then said, 'You speak real good English, and. . . .'

'You are wondering how it came about?'

'Yes, ma'am, ahh, I mean, Nita.'

'Missionaries. Once the Territories were filled with missionaries. They came here to convert the "Savage". They set up schools and churches. I went to one of those schools.'

'I see.'

Once more their gazes locked as Saracen was caught up in the allure of the woman before him. Suddenly he felt uncomfortable and cleared his throat. 'I'd better get going. Organize a few things before we leave in the morning.'

He made to leave and she blocked his path. She said, 'You are a strong man, Blaine Saracen.'

He felt his emotions stir. What was she doing? She was married.

Saracen swallowed hard and said, 'Goodnight, ma'am.'

He went to step around her, but this time when she blocked his path they became entangled in each other's arms. Before Saracen knew what was happening, Nita had started to kiss him and every part of his body seemed to come alive as he responded to a tenderness he'd never experienced before.

When they drew apart, Saracen wasn't sure what to say. It was Nita who spoke first. 'You will remember me now.'

'Hell yes,' Saracen blurted out. Then he gathered himself. 'What the hell was that? You're married.'

'To a weak fool,' Nita hissed as her expression changed.

Saracen frowned. 'I'm not sure what you mean. He faced down them Creeks today and shot it out with them.'

'Not in that way,' she explained. 'Do you know where he is at this moment?'

The scout shook his head.

Nita's voice was icy. 'He is with one of his many

whores. He has them all over Anson's.'

Saracen couldn't believe that any man would step out on Nita with another woman. She seemed mighty fine, and she was definitely easy on the eye.

He opened his mouth to say something, then closed it, not sure he could trust himself to say the right thing. When he did speak, he said deliberately, 'I have to go.'

This time Nita didn't try to stop him, and he hurried out the door.

The following morning was heavy with mist. It seemed to engulf the whole town like a giant white shroud. Saracen had the horses hitched and the prisoners in the tumbleweed wagon when Faraday emerged.

'Didn't you all sleep or something?' the deputy asked.

'Thought we'd get an early start,' the scout said.

'Damned still close to midnight,' Baron complained.

'Shut your hole,' Saracen snapped.

Faraday chuckled. 'You and me could work well together.'

Saracen scowled. 'Once we're back, I'm done. I ain't a lawman.'

'You're making a fine fist of it at the moment.'

The scout was about to say more when Nita Grey Elk appeared with a burlap sack filled with extra provisions. She handed it to Saracen and smiled at him.

'Don't forget to come back and visit,' she said softly.

The scout squirmed a touch as he took the food

and put it under the wagon seat. He turned back to face Nita and said, 'Thank you for the food.'

She reached out and touched his arm. 'You're welcome.'

Saracen glanced at Faraday who gave him a wry smile. 'Come on, Faraday,' he growled. 'Let's get out of here.'

They climbed aboard the wagon and started out of town. Beside him, Saracen could feel the deputy busting to speak. He shook his head, and snapped, 'Out with it before you blow up.'

'She's a good woman, that Nita.'

'What of it?'

'She deserves a man who treats her better than Henry does, that's for sure.'

'So?'

'Well. . . .'

'She's married, damn it.'

'Not so's you'd notice. Henry has more females in that town than he ought. I reckon he's bedded every second woman in that town, he's that bad.'

'Damn it, Faraday! Why are we even talking like this? I ain't looking for a woman. Especially one that's married already.'

'All right, forget I mentioned it.'

'Damn right I will.'

'Let's get back to Fort Smith then.'

'Yeah, let's.'

CHAPTER 4

Fort Smith Arkansas

Fort Smith was busy when the tumbleweed wagon rolled into town. The streets seemed to be full to over-flowing, and more than once Saracen had to almost stop the wagon or run someone down.

'What's going on?' Saracen asked. 'Where do all these people come from?'

Faraday looked about and gave a nod. 'The judge must be having a big hanging today.'

The deputy had grown stronger over the days and was all but ready for duty again. He spotted a man in the crowd and called out to him.

'Hey, Clem!' he shouted above the hum of excite-ment. 'What's going on?'

A man with large sideburns waved back to him and yelled, 'Judge Parker's hanging the whole of the Colby gang.'

'Glory be,' Faraday gasped. 'The judge is trying to outdo himself this time.'

'Who's Colby?' Saracen asked.

'He's a cold killer, that one. Rides with three others.

54

Last year he and his men killed a marshal over near Pawhuska in the Osage Territory. They'd just come down out of Kansas after robbing a bank. Bliss and me was part of a posse that tracked them, but we lost their trail when they doubled back on us and went north. After that, the judge put a big bounty on them. Looks like they was caught while we was away.'

'Hey, Faraday! Where's Bliss?' Clem shouted.

'Got shot!'

'No shit!'

'He'll live though!'

The man nodded and kept going.

They continued along until the crowd seemed to congregate and they could travel no further. Faraday stood on the wagon seat and fired two shots into the air. Folks turned to stare at the deputy who shouted as loud as he could.

'Move your asses out of the way. We got more business for the judge. All you folks is doing is blocking the road!'

With a few disgruntled cries, the crowd slowly parted until there was room enough for the wagon to proceed. Before long it was out the front of the courthouse, a single-storey affair with a high-pitched roof and a long veranda with stairs running up to it. It had windows along the front of it, and the jail cells were built underneath. Originally the building had served as the old fort's officers' barracks.

'Pull up over there and we'll unload them and put them in the cells. After that, we'll go and catch up with the judge.'

Saracen was only vaguely paying attention. Instead, his gaze was focused on the crowd gathered by the large gallows. The timber platform stood around seven feet off the ground, a solid oak crossbeam supported by two thick uprights. Affixed to the beam were six ropes, each with a noose fashioned at the end of it.

'Did you hear what I said?' asked Faraday.

Saracen turned his head to look at the deputy. 'He ever use all six of them things?'

Faraday nodded. 'Every now and then. Only be four today, though. I can't see him hanging anyone else with Colby and his killers.'

The wagon came to a halt and they both climbed down. The wagon lurched as they dismounted. Saracen took up his Winchester while Faraday unlocked the rear so Baron and his henchman could climb out. They were just about to walk down the steps to the iron door which led into the basement cells when the door swung open. A black marshal with a bushy moustache and short-cropped hair, a sawn-off shotgun in hand, climbed the stairs towards them. Behind him came four men.

'You all on gallows escort today, Bass?'

Deputy United States Marshal Bass Reeves stopped and stared at Faraday. 'My pleasure on this one, Amos. They done killed Lefty Singer when they was taken. I aim to see them swing good and high for it.'

'How about you stop your yap and get it done then, *boy*,' the first man in line snarled.

'All in good time, Colby.'

Faraday shook his head. 'Damn. They got old Lefty,

huh? Blasted shame.'

'He was a good man,' Reeves nodded. He glanced about. 'Say, where's Dan? I thought you two were out together.'

'Got hisself shot over at Anson's. He'll be OK. Just laid up for a while.'

Bass stared at Saracen. 'Who's the new man?'

'Name's Blaine Saracen,' the scout said and offered his right hand. 'And I ain't a new man.'

Reeves smiled and took it in a firm grip. 'Did Bliss deputize you?'

Saracen frowned. 'Yeah.'

Reeves' smile widened. 'Uh huh.'

The deputy turned back to Faraday. 'I'd best get these fellers up top, ready to swing. Catch up for a beer later?'

'Sure, why not?'

'You too, Saracen. The more the merrier.'

The scout watched the line saunter through the crowd towards the gallows.

'You want to watch?' Faraday asked.

'Nope. Seen a hanging once. Ghastly thing it was. Hangman was drunk, didn't do it right. Took the feller two full minutes to die.'

'Yeah. Can't say I'm overly fond of them myself. But sometimes killers deserve what they got coming. Come on, let's get Baron inside.'

As they walked down the steps, the stench was already apparent. But when the door opened it was like something surreal.

'Welcome to Hell, gentlemen,' Faraday said.

Saracen's guts turned over as the smell slapped him in the face. He fought the urge to throw up and Faraday must have noticed it.

He said, 'You get used to it after a couple of months. The judge has been lobbying for money to fix things up around here, but so far they ain't come across with any.'

Suddenly a filth-ridden form appeared beside the scout and clutched at his shirt.

'You gotta help me, mister,' the prisoner rasped. 'They're going to hang me in two days. They can't. I didn't do nothing. I'm innocent. Innocent, I tell you.'

Saracen shook off his hand and stepped back. Faraday, on the other hand, moved towards him and shoved him away.

'Get the hell away from us, Reynolds,' he snapped.

'But you gotta get me out of here.'

Saracen was about to speak when he was interrupted by the sound of gunfire from outside.

When Saracen and Faraday came clear of the top of the stairs they were faced with confusion. The crowd was a jumbled mess as it surged left and right. Through the chaos, he could make out the figures on top of the gallows. It looked as though the prisoners were free and one of them, Colby he thought, had a prisoner with a gun to his head.

On the platform lay a man dressed in black. The hangman, the scout guessed. Beside him, he heard Faraday gasp: 'The son of a bitch has got the judge.'

Saracen worked the lever on the Winchester and

said, 'Come on. Let's see if we can help.'

The closer they drew to the gallows, the more the crowd had thinned. By the time Saracen figured they were close enough, the crowd had dissipated and left five marshals behind, one of whom was dead and the other, Bass Reeves, wounded.

'One of you fellers best get me and my boys some horses or I swear I'm going to put a slug in this son of a bitch,' Colby growled.

'Just shoot them, damn it,' Parker said in a defiant voice.

'Shut your yap,' the outlaw snarled. 'They won't shoot. They know what'll happen if they do.'

Saracen watched on and adjusted his grip on the Winchester. He knew he could shoot Colby. He suspected most of them could, but it was the uncertainty of what would happen afterwards that stayed them all.

'Shoot, damn you!'

'Get the damned horses!' Colby shouted.

One of the marshals started to move and do as he was bid, but a deep voice stopped him. 'Stand fast, Quince,' Reeves ordered.

A cold shiver ran down Saracen's spine. If something wasn't done, Parker would die for certain because there would be no horses.

The scout raised his rifle and sighted along the barrel.

'What the hell are you doing?' Faraday gasped.

Saracen said, 'Just be ready.'

Colby directed his gaze at the scout. He snarled, 'I'll say this once. Put that gun down or I'll kill this old . . .'

The Winchester belched fire and the killer's head snapped back, a hole dead centre in his forehead. Without lowering the rifle, Saracen worked the lever and a fresh round rammed home. He squeezed the trigger again and the outlaw closest to the now dead Colby was thrust back. It was quick and violent.

Within a couple more heartbeats, the rest of the marshals had drawn their own guns and opened fire at the surviving killers, while Parker stood unmoving in the midst of it all.

When the sound of gun thunder died away, all of the Colby gang was down and dead. The judge stared down at them and shook his head. 'Damned fine waste of a hanging.'

He lifted his gaze and stared at Reeves. 'Are you OK, Bass?'

'I'm fine, Judge. It's just a flesh wound.'

Next, the steely gaze settled on Saracen. 'Who are you?'

'Blaine Saracen.'

Parker nodded at the badge. 'I don't recall you.'

'Bliss deputized him, Judge,' Faraday supplied.

'Where is Dan Bliss?'

'He got shot.'

Parker frowned. 'Is he dead?'

'Nope. Just laid up.'

The judge grunted. He said to Saracen, 'Give it an hour and then come see me in my office.'

The scout nodded.

'And don't be late. I can't abide tardiness. Make sure he ain't, Amos.'

'We'll be there, Judge.'

'Wouldn't mind having myself a bath first, wash some of the trail off.'

Parker still stood atop his gallows like some mythological god. 'Well, have one. Just don't be late.'

'Come on, Saracen,' Faraday said. 'I'll show you a place where you can be put up for a few days until you're ready to leave.'

The two started to walk away and Saracen asked, 'What place?'

'Boarding house that a few of us marshals use. It's run by a widow woman named Smith. Molly Smith.'

'I hope she ain't like the last woman I stayed with.'

Faraday smiled. 'Nope, she's a proper lady, this one.'

Faraday's words still rang in Saracen's ears as the woman ran hungry eyes over him and he swore, given half the chance, she would probably have eaten him whole.

The boarding house was on Hickory Street and was a white, double-storey construction that spoke money. Inside was even more lavish, with a chandelier in the entrance hall, a long staircase, wood panelling, polished furniture.

'Amos says you want a room, sweetie. I'm sure I can accommodate you. The one next to mine is empty.'

Good Lord.

Molly Smith was in her early forties, big-chested, slim waisted, and quite attractive with her long dark hair. But right at this point in time, the scout felt as though he was facing down a half-starved grizzly.

'I'll only need it for a couple of nights, ma'am.'

She smiled seductively. 'If you think a couple of nights is enough . . .'

'I'm sure it will be.'

Molly turned her gaze to Faraday. 'Would you show him to his room, Amos. I'll pour the man a bath. Can't have him going before the judge all smelly and dirt ridden.'

'Sure, Molly. I'll take care of it.'

'You could do with a bath yourself.'

Faraday held up his hands in self-defence. 'Oh, no. It ain't the start of the month yet. I'm still half clean.'

She wrinkled her nose. 'Yes, but the other half smells like a dead skunk.'

Faraday guffawed and slapped his thigh. 'Come on, Saracen. Let's get you to your room. I'd lock the door tonight if I was you.'

The scout was suddenly alarmed and Molly said, 'Why ever would he have to do such a thing?'

'People tend to sleep-walk around this place.'

Molly blushed a touch and watched them climb the stairs. She placed a hand across her ample bosom and gave a wry grin. She said in a quiet voice, 'Yes, they do.'

'Before we get started, gentlemen, I'd like to thank Mr Saracen here for what he did earlier,' Judge Isaac Parker began. 'If it wasn't for him, I guess I'd be dead by now.'

Saracen figured Parker to be somewhere in his early forties. He had dark, wavy hair and a dark goatee beard with a moustache. He'd arrived in Fort Smith in 1875 when he took up the position in the United States Court for the Western District of Arkansas.

Parker pointed at another man in the room who sat in a finely handcrafted chair. 'This, Mr Saracen, is William Henry Harrison Clayton. My chief prosecutor.'

Clayton took the scout's hand and they shook. 'Pleased to meet you, Saracen.'

'Likewise.'

The judge's office was well furnished and bright, helped by a large glazed window which caught a lot of sun. There were paintings on the walls and a healthy looking liquor cabinet which Faraday seemed to have his eye on.

Parker growled, 'Damn it, Amos, get yourself a damned drink before you die of thirst. I'll not have you mooning over it while we talk law work. Care for one, Mr Saracen?'

'I'm right thanks, Judge.'

They waited for Faraday to finish and then Parker started. 'Amos tells me you helped them out in Texas and then again in Anson's. Seems to me you were made to wear a badge, Mr Saracen.'

'Not me, Judge. I'm a scout. Plus I'm doing something else.'

Parker nodded and ignored the second part of the statement. 'Mighty handy skills to have for tracking down the outlaws and killers my marshals have to.'

'I'm here for a few days and then I'm gone.'

'Do you know the Nations, and Arkansas too?'

'I know the Nations. Arkansas I ain't too familiar with.'

Again, Parker nodded.

Parker's face grew stern. 'Dan Bliss deputized you, did he not?'

Saracen nodded.

'So you currently still work for me.'

The scout was wary. 'I guess you could say that.'

'I was aiming to send Bliss and Amos out on another job for me, but with Dan laid up I need a man to go with Amos. It might be too much for one man.'

'And you want me to go?'

'Well, officially you're still a deputy marshal.'

'I told Bliss I'd do it until we got them two prisoners back. No longer than that.'

'We could use you, Mr Saracen,' Parker persisted.

'No. I'm looking for my sister.'

'Where is she?'

'With Black Ted Allen.'

'Then she is already dead.'

'I'll find that out when I catch up with him.'

'And that's your last word?'

'Damn right it is. I'm sorry, Judge, but I have no wish to become a lawman,' he turned to Amos. 'Sorry, Amos.'

Faraday nodded. 'Hell, I don't blame you. Who wants to get shot at for twenty-five a month. One day we might even get a pay rise.'

Parker glared at him.

'Just saying, Judge.'

'Yeah, well. All right, Mr Saracen. We tried.'

The scout said, 'You did. Now, if we've finished, I'll be going.'

Parker said, 'Thank you for your help, Mr Saracen. If you change your mind you know where to find me. Good luck with finding your sister.'

'Thanks, Judge.'

Parker and Clayton remained silent as Saracen and Faraday left. Once they were gone, Parker turned to the prosecutor and said, 'I want him. I want him to go with Faraday.'

Clayton nodded. 'Consider it done.'

The Ace High Saloon wasn't your average establishment. It had a touch of class about it, with its long, hardwood bar with a polished counter, the huge mirror on the wall, rows of shelves, the brass foot rail, a large chandelier and the tastefully dressed whores. Whoever owned the place went to a lot of trouble to make it look better than the average western saloon.

Shame nobody told the patrons.

Saracen bellied up to the bar where he was greeted by a thin man in a striped shirt, covered by an apron. He looked at the newcomer and said, 'Howdy, mister. What'll it be?'

'Beer.'

The barkeep smiled and said, 'One beer, coming up.'

While he poured the ale, Saracen turned and ran his gaze across the room. He had to admit, it sure was nice.

The barkeep returned and placed the beer on the

counter. Saracen paid him and picked up his drink. He almost had it to his lips when a man with a big moustache and thin face bumped his arm, causing him to spill it.

'Why don't you watch what you're doing?' the man snapped.

Saracen glared at him. 'I could say the same thing, friend.'

'Who are you calling friend? I ain't your friend.'

'Fine. You ain't my friend.'

Saracen turned back towards the bar.

'Don't you damned well turn your back on me, you ornery son of a bitch,' the man hissed and grabbed Saracen's left shoulder to spin him around.

The scout had had enough. He let himself be spun instead of resisting. Once he had been turned all the way his right arm flashed out. At the end of it was his bunched fist. With an audible crack, knuckles struck home and the man reeled away, stunned.

He gathered himself and shook his head to rid himself of the cobwebs the blow had caused. He stared at Saracen and then, instead of coming straight back at him, the man smiled and peeled back his jacket lapel. Behind it was a marshal's badge.

'Attacking a federal officer of the law. I guess you're under arrest.'

Saracen's jaw dropped. 'You're kidding?'

'Well, well, well, Mr Saracen, we meet again,' Judge Isaac Parker smirked as he stared at Saracen. 'I hear tell that you attacked one of my marshals. A most

66

serious issue I'm afraid, Mr Saracen.'

Saracen glared at the judge. 'The son of a bitch baited me.'

Parker raised his eyebrows. 'He did? Why would he do that?'

'I don't know. But I'll find out.'

'You seem to forget, Mr Saracen, I have a prior claim.'

The scout's mouth snapped shut.

Parker's face clouded over and his voice grew hard. 'Did you assault my man or not?'

'I did. But not without provocation.'

'With or without, it doesn't much matter. You assaulted a federal lawman and as such you are looking at one year in the penitentiary.'

'One year!' Saracen exploded. 'You can't do that.'

'I can.'

'Christ almighty. It was just a harmless scrap.'

'Harmless or not, it happened. It's just a shame you weren't still a deputy. I might have been able to over-look it. Oh, well. That's the way it is sometimes.'

The scout shook his head.

'Unless, Mr Saracen, you are still a deputy marshal? Well?'

All of a sudden it dawned on him where it was going. 'You son of a bitch. I need to find my sister.'

'Take him away.'

'Wait!' Saracen held up his right hand. 'I'm still a deputy marshal.'

Parker nodded. 'Good. I'll see you and Amos later this afternoon. Case dismissed.'

'Judge?'

'Yes, Mr Saracen?'

'You're still a son of a bitch.'

'I know, Mr Saracen, I know.'

'You will leave tomorrow, gentlemen,' Parker told them.

'Where for?' Faraday asked.

Saracen looked down at the star pinned to his chest. All of a sudden it felt as though it weighed a good fifty pounds heavier than it should.

'In the mountains south-east of here, there is a town called Devlin's Peak. Have you heard of it?'

Faraday nodded. 'Yes, sir. Old Frank Bell is the sheriff there.'

'That's the place. He has a prisoner he wants out of there. I'm going to try him and have him swing if required. Save him going to the trouble.'

'Who is the prisoner?' Saracen asked.

'Drake Belden.'

'Oh, Christ!' Faraday exclaimed. 'Craig Belden's son.'

'And if he gives you any trouble, bring him in, too. I've been looking for a reason to hang him.'

'Who is Craig Belden?' Saracen asked.

'The mayor of Devlin's Peak. He's bad news. We're reasonably sure he had a feller killed last year, and maybe one not very long ago. Bliss tried to nail him, but couldn't turn up any hard evidence on him. His son apparently killed a young lady over there. The sheriff has him locked away, but you'll need to find some witnesses while you're at it. Ask questions and the like.'

'Should we expect trouble?'

Parker nodded. 'And then some. You do what you have to, but you hang on to that prisoner. You shoot anyone who tries to take him from you. Understood?'

Saracen nodded. 'Anything else we should know about?'

'Isn't that enough?'

'I don't know. Maybe there's some army you forgot to mention or something like it?'

'Sarcasm does not become you, Deputy Marshal Saracen.'

'Neither does death,' Saracen snapped.

'Nor should it,' Parker retorted. 'So you should remain alive. Your death would inconvenience me somewhat.'

'I'll see what I can do.'

'One last thing, Mr Saracen. If I or any of my marshals hear of Allen, I'll let you know.'

'Thanks.'

CHAPTER 5

Kent, Arkansas

Black Ted Allen and his band of no-goods rode into Kent that same afternoon. There were six of them in all: Allen, the scar-faced, unshaven bear himself, then a slim Texan named Bodie, Henshaw, the baby-faced killer from Kansas, Eriksonn the Swede, and Walker and Pete who both hailed from parts unknown. As their horses slopped along the muddy street the riders had their sights set on the Kent Bank, where reportedly a tidy sum of ten thousand dollars was being held.

As they rode, Allen took note of the townsfolk on the boardwalks. He didn't like it. He'd planned on robbing the bank early that morning as it opened, but things had happened and now they were late. It was around noon and the town was busy.

The riders rode up to the bank and stopped at the hitch rail. Across the street behind them, Allen had noticed the jail. Not ideal. They climbed down from their horses, and as he walked past Bodie, Allen said, 'Take Pete across the street and take care of the law.'

Bodie smiled, 'Sure.'

Allen grabbed his arm before he could move away. 'Don't shoot anyone until we're finished at the bank.'

The outlaw smiled again. 'Sure.'

'I mean it.'

The two men started across the street and stopped abruptly when a rider cut across in front of them. He was a solidly built man with a large moustache. He seemed not to see them, but they, on the other hand, saw him. Especially the marshal's badge pinned to his vest.

They both let their hands drop to their six-guns, half expecting the rider to stop and do the same. Instead, he kept on riding.

They glanced back at Allen. He hadn't noticed and was already climbing the steps on to the boardwalk. Bodie shrugged and the pair kept walking.

Four grime-covered men, dressed in not much more than rags, and armed to the teeth. What more could spell bank hold-up? And when they entered the Kent bank, Elias Morgan, manager, felt the blood drain from his face and his knees begin to tremble.

The well-dressed man reached under the counter-top and rested his quivering hand on the butt of the Peacemaker he kept there. He desperately wanted to bring it up, thumb back the hammer, and shoot the outlaw as he approached the counter, but the Colt had grown so heavy he couldn't lift it.

Allen shouldered an elderly woman in a cream-coloured dress aside, whom Morgan was serving, and while she protested his rudeness, the outlaw boss thumped his six-gun down on the polished top and gave him a cruel smile: 'I'd like to make a withdrawal.'

The woman gasped, and the manager noticed that the three men who'd entered with Allen had spread out across the dimly lit room and drawn their own weapons. One of them used his six-gun to knock down a male customer, Miller the telegrapher.

He fell in a heap on the floor and moaned. The outlaw bent down and hit him again. There was a sickening crunch as his jaw broke, but it had the desired effect. Miller ceased to move or make a sound. The other customers in the room, another woman and two men, were immediately silent.

Morgan stared at the cold eyes and stammered, 'I . . . I. . . .'

Allen picked up his Colt and thumbed back the hammer. He pointed it at the manager's face and snapped, 'What you'd best be saying is "yes, sir".'

Morgan swallowed. 'Yes, sir.'

'Good. Open the safe.'

'I . . .'

The fist with the Colt in it streaked forward and rose just a fraction. The gun butt hit Morgan across the bridge of the nose and made him stagger back.

'Now!' Allen barked. 'Henshaw, give this son-of-a-bitch a hand.'

'No problem,' the baby-faced killer Henshaw growled and made his way round the end of the counter and in behind it. He dragged Morgan to his feet by his hair and to the back of the room where the safe was.

Allen turned back and stared at Eriksonn. 'How's it look outside?'

The Swede peeked out through the front window and then said, '*Ja, gut.*'

'Let's hope it stays that way.'

That's when gunfire erupted from the jail across the street.

When Bodie and Pete entered the jail, they found Willard Groves pouring himself a cup of steaming black coffee.

'What can I do for you gents?' the grey-haired lawman asked as he replaced the banged-up coffee pot back on the stove top.

Bodie's Schofield came free of its holster and he thumbed the hammer back. 'You can keep your hand away from that hog-leg in your holster, for a start.'

Groves frowned. 'What is this?'

'Shut your yap, old man,' Pete snapped and relieved Groves of his holstered six-gun and tucked it into his belt.

Bodie motioned to the chair and said, 'Sit down.'

Still holding the steaming hot cup, Groves walked over to his desk and sat. He placed the cup on the desk but never let it go.

'So, what now? Who are you, anyway?'

Pete smiled at Bodie. 'You think we should tell him?'

The slim Texan rubbed at his square jaw. 'Way I figure it, don't really matter much.'

Pete moved closer to the front of the desk and

placed both hands on it. He leaned forward and stared hard into Groves' eyes. 'We're part of the Black Ted Allen gang.'

The sheriff's face remained passive.

Pete snorted with disgust. 'What? Nothing to say?'

'What do you want me to say? Please don't shoot me? I have a family?'

'Might be a start.'

While Groves sat there he was certain he would never see the day out. He shook his head. 'Nope. I ain't going to give you what you want. What you deserve, however, I can help you with.'

Pete looked confused and straightened up. 'Huh?'

The battered desktop exploded outwards and upwards with a tremendous roar. Razor-sharp wooden splinters combined with small lead pellets from the sawn-off shotgun fixed beneath the heavy timber structure scythed through the air. The deadly mix ripped into Pete's head and chest, rendering him unrecognizable in a heartbeat.

Groves lurched to his feet as he tore the weapon free and brought it up to fire the last barrel.

Bodie overcame his shock at the sudden violence of the situation and his six-gun snapped into line. He squeezed the trigger before the second charge of buckshot could cut him in half.

The slug burned deep into Groves' chest, knocking him back. He staggered and turned the chair over behind him. Another slug from Bodie punched him back against the wall, pinning him there briefly before he slid to the floor.

Bodie glanced down at the bloody mess that had once been Pete and knew straightaway that the outlaw was dead. He cursed under his breath and headed for the door. Allen wasn't going to be happy.

'Get that goddamned safe open,' Allen snarled. 'Christ almighty. Swede, get out there and make sure no one gets near the horses. Walker, you too.'

They disappeared out the door and left Henshaw and Allen to finish up. In what seemed to take an age, Morgan managed to get the safe opened. Henshaw loaded up the bags the outlaws had brought with them and then stood erect. He smiled at the manager, tipped his hat, then gutshot him on the spot.

'All done, Ted,' he said as he walked round the end of the counter.

The scar-faced killer nodded and turned to their prisoners, who cowered in the corner. His mouth curved up in a cold grin and he unblinkingly opened fire with his Colt. When he had finished, he turned and walked towards the door.

When Allen emerged from the bank he paused on the boardwalk. The town was already starting to rally at the sound of the gunfire. Men emerged from different stores along the street with weapons in hand.

As the outlaw leader calmly started to reload his gun he barked orders. 'Henshaw, get them sacks on my horse. Walker, Eriksonn, shoot anyone who has a gun.'

He paused. Then, 'Hell, just shoot anyone. Clear the damn street.'

'Sure thing, Ted,' Walker said.

Allen snapped the loading gate shut and glanced up and saw Bodie. 'What the hell happened?'

'Sheriff had a shotgun under his desk,' Bodie explained as he climbed atop his horse.

'Where's Pete?'

'He's dead.'

'Shit!' Allen growled. 'Let's get the hell out of here.'

Suddenly the street erupted in violence. The Swede and Walker began picking out targets methodically on the street. By the time they were all mounted, the pair had put down three townsfolk, and the good citizens of Kent were starting to fight back.

Lead filled the air, and Walker grunted when a slug from an old Spencer carbine punched into his guts. On its way in, it clipped his belt buckle. The misshapen hunk of lead tore at everything it touched. Flesh, sinew, intestines, everything. It blew out his back in a spray of blood and gore.

The outlaw doubled over and dropped his six-gun. He grabbed at the saddle-horn to keep himself from falling.

'Ted, Walker's hit!' Henshaw exclaimed.

Allen swung his mount and glanced at the wounded man. He swore vehemently and snarled, 'Leave him.'

'We can't leave him like that!' Bodie cried out above the gunfire.

Allen moved his horse in beside Walker's, raised his six-gun and shot the wounded outlaw in the head. 'You happy now?'

'Damn it!' Bodie shouted, spurring his horse hard. The animal leaped forwards and was at top speed before it had gone ten strides.

The rest of the outlaws fell in behind him, and as they fled Kent, more shots rang out hard on their heels.

Devlin's Peak, Arkansas

The sun sank below the western horizon that evening, its blood-red fingers reaching out across the Arkansas sky, an ominous cloud settling over the town of Devlin's Peak. And none felt it more than Sheriff Frank Bell.

'Tonight's the night, old man,' Drake Belden sneered. 'There's no way you'll see morning. My old man will see to that.'

Bell had been a lawman in Devlin's Peak for fifteen years. A lawman for longer. Now, with his hair more white than dark, his rheumatism playing up of a cold morning and his eyesight growing weaker, he knew his time was about up. Not because of his age, but because the kid was right. Craig Belden was going to kill him and break his son out of jail. He just wished that the marshals had arrived sooner.

The old sheriff frowned. By hell, he would make him pay for it. He walked across the small room to the gun rack and grabbed down a Winchester. He took it across to his battered desk, opened the top drawer, and took out a box of cartridges. Once the carbine was loaded, he headed for the door.

'You running away, Bell? Lost your spine?'

77

Bell stopped and turned. 'I ain't going far, kid. I'll just be outside waiting for your old man to show.' He patted the carbine. 'Got me a bullet right in here with his name on it.'

The sheriff walked out the door, ignoring the string of expletives that the younger Belden hurled after him. He stood on the boardwalk, looking up and down the darkened thoroughfare. A few lights illuminated the boardwalk planks and cast shadows across others. Noise erupted from further along the street at the Pine Oak Saloon. Opposite to where he stood, and a couple of buildings along to the right was the newspaper office. The light was on, and Bell figured that Merriweather the editor was preparing his printing press for the following morning.

'Damn Craig Belden to hell,' Bell snapped.

The Ouachitas

Faraday cleaned up the plates and poured himself and Saracen a cup of strong black coffee. The fire crackled and they sat close to it to make the most of its warmth. After the sun had gone down, a chill had swiftly enveloped the rugged landscape. The former scout leaned forwards and poked at the fire with a stick. The flames flared and the coals gave off a renewed heat.

Since they'd left Fort Smith the day before, they'd managed to cover a good distance despite the terrain. Faraday gave Saracen his coffee and asked, 'What's she like?'

Saracen looked up from the fire and said, 'Who? My sister?'

'Yeah.'

Blaine stared into the flames. 'She's the most kind-hearted person I know. She's younger than me by four years. She'd been married once, but her husband was killed when his horse fell on him. Devastated her. She moved back home after that. Almost as tall as me though, she is.' He shrugged. 'Well, she was the last time I saw her.'

Faraday sat down on the other side of the campfire. 'How long ago was that?'

'Five years. Before I went to Arizona. I'd been up in northern Texas scouting for the cavalry against the Comanche. Spent a month with them before I left.'

'I'm sorry,' Faraday said.

'It ain't your fault, Amos.'

'I know. I just felt like it should be said.'

Saracen nodded.

'You been searching for Allen and your sister ever since you found out?'

'Yeah. You'd think someone like him would be easy to track down. But ever since he left Texas last year, everything has been quiet.'

'You know there's a good chance she ain't still alive, don't you?'

The nod was almost imperceptible. 'Yeah.'

Silence descended upon them and it lasted for a time before Saracen asked. 'Tell me about Belden.'

'The judge has been after him for a while. But the son of a bitch is as slippery as a fish. But like all fish, if you feed them the right bait, they hook themselves. Which I'm thinking the arrest of his son will accomplish.'

79

'I'm starting to think I should have taken jail.'

Faraday threw the dregs of his coffee on to the ground. 'Could have been a wiser choice. Next time you might want to take it.'

'Maybe there won't be a next time.'

Fort Smith, Arkansas

There was a knock at the door and Judge Isaac Parker looked up from his scribing. He frowned. Who on earth could that be at this time of night? 'Come.'

The door opened and the lamp flickered with the sudden rush of cold air. Bass Reeves entered and closed the door. Parker raised his eyebrows and said, 'Good lord man, what are you doing out at this time of night?'

Reeves held up a folded piece of paper. 'A telegram came in, Judge. Bad news I'm afraid.'

'Really? What is it this time?'

'Black Ted Allen. Robbed the Kent bank and killed a bunch of people.' He handed over the note, and while the judge started to read it, continued: 'They're headed towards the Nations. I have a feeling there might be another reason why they're headed there.'

'The Katy?' Parker guessed.

The Katy was the Missouri-Kansas-Texas railroad, shortened to the 'K-T' or the 'Katy'.

Reeves nodded. 'I do recall something coming through over the wire about a money shipment on board one of the trains in the next week or so.'

Parker knew Reeves was right. He'd heard the same thing. 'OK, Bass. Wake them all up. I want every man that can be spared, out there patrolling the line. Allen has to be stopped before he can cross it into the Nations. If he gets in there we'll play hell digging him out. Just in case he slips through, have someone inform the Indian Police.'

'Sure thing, Judge. What about Saracen? I heard he was looking for Allen.'

'Saracen is busy. I ain't got time or men to spare chasing all over Arkansas after him. Do what I asked you to.'

'Yes, sir.'

CHAPTER 6

Devlin's Peak, Arkansas

The town was quiet. Too quiet. And it wasn't until they reached the jail that Saracen and Faraday found out why.

They had reached the town on the third day of traversing the rugged trail through the Ouachitas. It was mid-afternoon when they came over the low ridge and saw the town laid out in a broad clearing surrounded by tall trees and distant rock formations.

The tumbleweed wagon rattled to a halt beside Saracen. 'There she is. Devlin's Peak.'

Saracen noticed him lean down and pick up his sawn-off messenger gun.

'You ain't expecting to use that thing, are you?' he asked.

He spat a glob of tobacco juice over the side of the conveyance and said, 'Never can be too careful.'

The former scout shook his head and mumbled something under his breath.

'What you say?' Faraday asked.

'I said remind me to shoot Parker when we get

back,' Saracen growled as he adjusted his Schofield. He leaned forward in the saddle and took out the Winchester from the scabbard. 'I might as well have stayed fighting Apaches. Seems to me it might have been safer.'

'Then how would you find your sister?' Faraday pointed out.

With a suddenly sombre face, Saracen said, 'Yeah. Come on then, let's get this done. I want to be back on the trail before dark.'

'What? And forgo all of the lovely pleasures Devlin's Peak has to offer?'

'There's only one pleasure you want that you'll find down there,' Saracen said.

Faraday smiled at him. 'You sure you ain't been here before?'

Saracen ignored him and edged his mount onwards along the rutted trail. Behind him, he heard the slap of reins and the wagon creak as it lurched forwards.

'Just be ready, is all I can say,' Faraday called after him. 'Just be ready.'

Faraday leaned over the side of the wagon and spat on the street. 'Shit! I wasn't expecting that.'

'Explains why the town is so quiet.'

The grim expressions on both their faces said it all as they stared at the body of Sheriff Frank Bell. A gust of wind caught it and the ripening corpse swayed gently. By the colour and smell of the exposed flesh, Saracen figured it had been there for a couple of days.

He climbed down from the saddle and stepped up

on the boardwalk. Whoever had hung Bell from the awning in front of the jail had picked the strongest cross-member they could find.

Inside Saracen found what he'd expected. The jail cells were empty. He snorted in disgust and turned and walked out. Once on the boardwalk, he looked at Faraday. 'Find the undertaker. Get the poor old bastard cut down. He don't deserve to be left hanging like that.'

'What are you going to do?'

'Find out what happened.'

'How do you propose to do that?' Faraday asked curiously.

'Who is the one person in a town this size that knows everything that happens?' Saracen asked him.

After giving his answer some thought, the deputy marshal said, 'Newspaperman.'

Saracen stepped down from the boardwalk and started across the street. 'Exactly.'

The former scout crossed over and climbed the steps on to the other boardwalk. There were a few more people on the street, and he figured word had started to spread that marshals were in town.

He opened the door and found a thin-faced man with wire-rimmed glasses, waiting for him behind a counter. 'I've been waiting for you.'

Saracen turned and glanced out the large front window. It acted like a large frame in which hung the corpse of the dead sheriff. He turned back. 'The name's Saracen. Deputy Marshal out of Fort Smith.'

'Why couldn't you lot have been here three days

ago?' the man snapped.

'What's your name?'

'Merriweather,' he growled.

'We're here now. Tell me what happened.'

Merriweather's voice dripped with sarcasm. 'What do you think happened? They murdered him, that's what happened.'

'Who did it?'

'Belden's men. They came to break his son out of jail the other night and thought it would be fun to hang Frank Bell while they were at it.'

'Was Belden with them?'

Merriweather shook his head. 'No. He wouldn't be seen to be mixed up with something like that. It might get him in trouble with the law. Fine, upstanding citizen that he is. But he sure gave the order for it to be done.'

Saracen nodded. 'Where's his son? Where's Drake?'

'Probably crawled back under the rock he came out from. The bastard helped them do it.'

'Will you testify in court to that fact?' Saracen asked.

The newspaperman paled. 'You've got to be kidding. And wind up swinging at the end of a rope like Sheriff Bell? Not likely.'

Saracen grew angry. 'Is the rest of the town like you?'

'How do you mean?'

'Full of hot air and bluster until they have to do something about it. No wonder Bell swung from the rope. The whole spineless town refused to back him.'

'You don't live here,' Merriweather pointed out.

'You have no idea what it's like.'

'What are the names of those who did it?' Saracen asked.

Merriweather looked out the window and his eyebrows raised. 'What are they doing?'

The former scout turned and saw Faraday and the undertaker cutting the body down. 'They're doing what should have been done days ago.'

'No, no, no. He said it had to stay there.'

'Who?'

'Drake Belden. He said he'd shoot anyone who took it down. It was to remind the whole town who was in charge.'

'He's in for a shock then, ain't he. Now, tell me some names.'

Merriweather hesitated. Then, 'Ward Smith, Joe Bond, Cal Mertens and Chick Bennett.'

'I've heard of a couple of them,' Saracen said. 'Bond was a bounty hunter who used to haunt the border regions. Mertens was wanted in Arizona for bank robbery.'

The newspaperman said, 'That's right. The other two are just as bad. Ward Smith is a hired gun from Kansas, and Chick Bennett considers himself a fast gun but the only time it seems to be fast is when the other feller is facing away from him. Oh, God. There's two of them now.'

Saracen stared out the window and saw the two men approaching Faraday and the undertaker. One was slim, tall. The other was a touch rounder but still tall. 'Who are they?'

'The thin one is Bennett. The other is Mertens.'

The ex-scout started towards the door. 'Wait here.'

'I ain't going anywhere.'

By the time Saracen's feet touched the hard-packed earth of the main street once again, he knew there would be trouble. Especially when he heard a voice say, 'You were told to put it back up.'

'Are you hard of hearing?' Faraday asked them. 'I'm a Deputy United States Marshal. See the badge?'

The thin man shook his head. 'Nope. I don't see nothing. Drake Belden says it has to stay there, so it stays.'

'And I say it gets buried,' Saracen told them with a steady voice.

They turned to face him and noted the Winchester pointed in their direction. 'Who are you?'

'Deputy United States Marshal Blaine Saracen.'

Bennett snorted. 'Another one.'

'What do you want to do, Chick?' Mertens asked.

'Maybe someone should teach them it ain't nice to interfere with things that ain't got nothing to do with them.'

Saracen's grip tightened on the Winchester. He said, 'Amos, did that sound like a threat to you?'

'Sure did,' Faraday agreed.

'Thought so.'

Saracen's move was so fast that Bennett already had a bullet in his chest before he could move an inch. The Winchester came up level and the ex-scout squeezed the trigger. With a roar, it bucked in his hands. The muzzle spat flame and Bennett was flung violently back.

Saracen levered another round into the breech and centred the carbine on Mertens. The killer clutched at the butt of his New Model Remington. Before he could clear leather, the Winchester bucked again.

The .45-.70 slug punched into Mertens' guts just above his belt buckle. He hunched over and slumped to his knees. He raised his head to stare at Saracen. With gritted teeth, he snarled, 'You gut shot me, you son of a bitch.'

The lever on the Winchester worked again. The killer stared Saracen in the eye and through the pain which radiated outward from the savage wound, he hawked and spat, narrowly missing Saracen's boots.

The hammer fell and Mertens died with a bullet in his brain.

'Holy Hannah,' Faraday blurted out. 'You are something with that Winchester. You that fast with the Schofield?'

'Only if I have to be.'

He glanced at the trembling undertaker. 'Sorry about that. But you've got a couple of extra customers.'

'Ah . . . yes, sir,' the man in black stammered.

Crowds had begun to form on both sides of the street, drawn out by the sound of gunfire. Saracen ran a curious gaze over them, noting the concern on most of their faces. He caught the sound of someone say, 'Now they've done it.'

Another said, 'Dead men they are.'

Never before had Saracen seen a town so petrified

of its own shadow. He walked over to Faraday and said, 'They're all scared.'

'Yeah. It's worse than I figured it would be. I think the lynching of the sheriff saw to that.'

'What the hell is going on here?' a voice boomed.

Both deputies turned to face a large man dressed in a black suit with a string tie. His hair had started to grey, and his face had the makings of deep lines on it. Craig Belden!

Beside him were two other men. One was dressed much like a cowhand, the other, however, was dressed in black and wore twin six-guns. This had to be Ward Smith, the other man, Joe Bond.

Belden saw the two men on the ground and seemed slightly shaken by it. He gathered himself and glared at Saracen and Faraday. 'Who are you two?'

Saracen said, 'Like you don't already know. You saw the tumbleweed wagon.'

Belden's voice grew icy. 'I meant your names?'

'I'm Saracen, he's Faraday. We're here for your son.'

Belden smirked. 'He ain't here.'

'No shit. Where is he?'

Belden shrugged his broad shoulders. 'Who knows? You wasted your time coming all the way here. Now you can leave.'

'Hah!' Faraday guffawed. 'We're only just getting started. Your son killed a woman and we aim to take him back to be hung.'

The Devlin's Peak mayor forced another smile. 'All lies. My advice to you is to leave. Go back to Fort

Smith. We can take care of things from here. Why, we're even holding an election tomorrow for the office of sheriff.'

Saracen was sceptical. 'Really?'

'Really. Ward here has already put himself forward for the job. Once he's elected, then he'll take care of what needs to be done.'

'Uh huh,' Saracen grunted. 'Amos, what would Judge Parker say if we returned to Fort Smith without our prisoner?'

'I think he'd be a might upset about it all.'

'I agree. And what was it he said if anyone interfered with us carrying out our sworn duty?'

The mirthless grin on Faraday's face grew large. 'He basically said we could shoot them.'

Saracen's gaze grew cold. 'You get that, Mr Belden. If you or any of your men try to stop us from doing our job, there'll be hell to pay.'

'So that's the way it's going to be, is it?'

'Sure is.'

'Then I wish you luck,' Belden said and turned away.

'What now?' Faraday asked.

'We'll get settled in here and then in the morning, we'll start asking around about Drake Belden.'

'He could be miles away by then,' Faraday grumbled.

'I don't think so. If they ain't afraid to kill a sheriff, somehow I don't think they're going to run away. I think they'll be planning their next move.'

'Which is?'

'How they're going to kill us.'

Craig Belden poured himself a drink with a trembling hand. Some of the brownish-coloured whiskey spilled on to the polished desktop when the glass overflowed. His son Drake sat on a lounge against a striped wall-papered wall. 'Let me take care of them, Pa. They'll be dead by morning.'

'I should let them take you, is what I should do,' Belden snarled at him. The marshal called Saracen had him worried, and he didn't like it one bit.

The small lamp on the side table in the far corner of the room cast a low orange glow across the room already dimmed by dark timber furniture. In the ensuing silence following Belden's outburst, the tick of an upright clock sounded almost deafening.

'I can do it, Pa,' Drake persisted.

'Oh, shut up!' his father snapped. 'Ward, what do you think?'

'We could kill them,' Smith allowed. 'But it would only breed more of them. Might be best if we let things die down and hope that they go away when they can't find Drake.'

'I ain't hiding like a yellow cur,' Drake snapped.

'You'll do as you're told, boy,' his father shot back. 'I think Ward is right. For the time being, we wait.'

The Nations, next morning
'Get the hell up, you lot,' Allen growled. 'We've got miles to make today.'

The outlaws started to roll out of their blankets and

cursed the early morning cold. They'd slipped across into the Nations under the cover of darkness the night before, after having to dodge a couple of marshals patrolling the line.

'We need supplies,' Bodie pointed out. 'We've got stuff all between us.'

'What do you want me to do about it?'

'Anson's Post ain't far from here,' Henshaw said.

Allen rolled his eyes. 'What about the Cherokee Lighthorse, idiot?'

'They're only Indians,' Henshaw said. 'They don't count for much. If they give us trouble we can shoot them.'

'No, get some bacon on and cooking.'

'We ain't got any,' Eriksonn told him. 'I said yesterday.'

'Fine, coffee will do then.'

'Ain't got any of that, either,' Bodie answered.

'Damn it. All right, then. We'll stop over in Anson's and get some supplies before we head north. We've got a couple of days before we meet up with Hank and his boys and the train is due.'

The 'Hank' whom Allen talked about was Hank Bowdrie. Another cold-hearted outlaw like Allen.

'Hey, do you suppose he's still got that woman from Texas with him? The one you sold to him? She'd be one to keep a man warm on these cold nights.'

'I guess you'll find out, won't you?'

Bodie grinned. 'I guess I will.'

CHAPTER 7

Devlin's Peak, Arkansas

Saracen sipped his coffee and stared across the street in a trance. He was thinking about Victoria, about when they were younger how one of the boys from Largo had kissed her and she'd been so shocked she started to run home, forgetting that they had all gone to town that morning together.

Saracen had seen her go, luckily enough, and he took off after her on his horse. She'd been fifteen at the time. When he found out what had happened he rode back towards town to find the boy responsible. He found him outside the dry goods store. But Victoria had chased him all the way back, pleading with him not to hurt him. She married the boy four years later. Twelve months after that, he was dead.

Faraday emerged from the office and stood there.

'I'm headed back over to the newspaper office after,' Saracen said. 'Do you want to get around town and see what you can come up with?'

'Sure.'

'Just be careful.'

A young woman with long dark hair started to cross the street and head in their direction. Saracen watched her approach. She climbed the steps and stopped in front of them both. She said, 'My name is Olivia Parmenter.'

They just stared at her while she did the same, like her name was meant to mean something to them.

'April was my sister.'

It still meant nothing to them.

'The girl that Drake Belden murdered.'

It hit them between the eyes. Saracen apologized. 'I'm sorry, ma'am, we weren't told your sister's name. We were kind of expecting the sheriff to still be alive when we got here.'

She nodded. 'Yes.'

'Can you tell us anything at all about the . . .' Saracen hesitated, then, 'about what happened?'

'My sister and Drake were out walking. She'd been having second thoughts about marrying him. She was to tell him that night. He claims she never did. He also claims that she left him to walk home on her own. Something she's never done before. He always escorted her to the door before he went home himself.'

'So what changed?' Faraday asked her.

She shook her head. 'Nothing. He killed her.'

'OK.'

'Her body was found' – she took a deep breath before continuing – 'was found near the corrals at the edge of town. She'd been strangled.'

'And you're convinced it was Drake Belden

because. . . ?' Saracen asked.

'When Doctor Murphy examined my sister, she had blood under her fingernails. When Sheriff Bell found out, he forced Drake to remove his shirt at gunpoint. The scratches were plain to see. When the doctor examined them, he agreed that they were scratches. Drake was locked up straightaway. Now he's escaped, and Sheriff Bell is dead.'

Saracen nodded apologetically. 'I'm sorry for your loss, ma'am. You wouldn't know where he'd most likely be hiding out, would you?'

She shook her head. 'No.'

The ex-scout looked at Faraday. 'I guess we'll have to find him the hard way.'

Olivia's shoulders slumped. 'I'm afraid that even if you do find him, you'll never get him out of town before Craig Belden's men kill you.'

'They tried yesterday,' Faraday pointed out. 'Didn't do them any good.'

'He's not one to give up easy.'

'Neither are we. Go home, Miss Parmenter. We'll find the man who killed your sister.'

'I hope you do, marshal. I sure hope you do.'

Merriweather looked up from what he was doing when Saracen entered the newspaper office, and he grimaced. He thought maybe he was done with the marshal, but obviously not.

'What can I do for you, Marshal Saracen?'

'Information.'

He went back to what he was doing and said, 'I

don't know anything.'

'You're just going to let Drake Belden get away with murder, is that it?'

'If it means I stay alive.'

'Where might he be hiding out?'

'I don't know.'

'Come on, man, you run the local newspaper, you know everything that goes on in town.'

'In this case, I don't. Besides, he's probably long gone.'

Saracen sighed. Merriweather was holding something back. He moved around the counter and approached him. The newspaperman rose from his chair and backed up a step as the sound of boots on boards grew closer.

'If you were Drake Belden, Merriweather, and someone was after you, where would you hide?'

The newspaperman wanted to say 'I don't know' so bad it was etched on his face. Before he could, however, Saracen took another step forwards. 'The sawmill.'

'What sawmill?'

'About three miles south of here. Just follow the trail. Craig Belden owns a sawmill. There are some cabins out there that the woodcutters use when they don't come into town. If he's anywhere, then that would be it.'

Saracen patted Merriweather on the shoulder. 'That wasn't hard now, was it?'

Saracen left the trail and halted his horse inside the

edge of the tree line where he could sit and watch the sawmill from the low ridge.

He figured there were at least ten men working the mill itself. Occasionally a horse team would drag a log out of the forest to be milled. Further up some of the surrounding slopes were large bare patches that had once been covered in large stands of timber. The surrounds of the mill itself were a churned-up mass of bare earth. Saracen could only imagine what it would be like when it rained.

Off to the right of the mill were three long buildings made from logs. Saracen figured they'd be the quarters for the workmen. If Drake Belden was down there, then that was where he'd be. Maybe he should have brought Faraday with him. Though he was busy doing other things. Too late now, he thought, as he urged his mount forwards.

By the time he hit the outskirts of the mill the steel-grey skies overhead had opened to let a fine mist drift down. Just enough to be a pain.

He kept riding until he was stopped by a large man wearing a slicker which hung down to his knees. His trousers were cut off above the tops of his heavy boots, and the drizzle, which was getting heavier, dripped from the brim of his felt hat.

He stared at Saracen and asked, 'What brings you here' – he caught a glimpse of the badge – 'Marshal?'

'Who are you?' Saracen asked.

'Butler, foreman,' Butler told him.

'Uh huh.' Saracen noticed that more men were starting to gather, some holding axes. 'I'm looking for

Drake Belden.'

Butler feigned nonchalance. 'He ain't here.'

The ex-scout ran his gaze over the newcomers, reading the open hostility on their faces. His eyes came back to Butler. 'Mind if I look around?'

'Yeah, I do,' he challenged.

'Maybe I'll just look anyway.'

A shrug. 'Have it your way.'

Saracen climbed down, all the while keeping an eye on the timber men. He led his horse towards the three buildings. They followed along at a distance, but none moved to interfere. The drizzle grew into rain, heavier but not soaking. He opened the door of the first cabin and stepped inside. Apart from bunks, a large table and a pot-belly stove, it was empty.

The second was much the same. When he opened the door of the third and stepped in, he was hit up the side of the head by something hard.

Saracen fell to his knees, his head swimming like a whirlpool. He grabbed at the Schofield but it felt like a lead weight in his weakened state. The moment before everything went black, Saracen cursed himself for being a fool. And if he lived through this, he'd never make the same mistake again.

Butler looked at the grinning face of Drake Belden, who said, 'Go and get my father. He'll want to be here when this bastard gets what's coming to him.'

Anson's Post, Choctaw Nation

Johnny Hawkfeather watched the outlaws ride into Anson's Post and straightaway he recognized Allen.

Not from a 'Wanted' poster, but from first-hand experience. He'd come across Allen up in Cherokee Territory.

The outlaw and the rest of his gang had robbed a bank in Kansas. Hawkfeather had been in a small settlement called Lightning Creek, settled in 1869 by members of the Eastern Delaware tribe. When Allen and his men had hit the town, they'd created bloody murder when one of his men had made advances towards a Delaware woman. Her husband had taken offence to the act and he'd struck the outlaw.

The outlaw's response had been to shoot the husband dead. What followed was etched in Hawkfeather's mind forever. The rest of the gang, Allen included, had commenced shooting down people indiscriminately. By the time they'd ridden out of Lightning Creek, five people were dead and seven wounded. Now he was here in Anson's Post.

Hawkfeather watched the outlaws make their way along to the new trading post which had been built just before the old one was converted. Once they'd disappeared inside, he hurried along to find Henry Grey Elk.

It was Nita who answered the knock. 'What is it, Johnny Hawkfeather? My husband is not home if that is who you want?'

'I need to find him. I saw some bad white men ride into town.'

Nita's voice was bitter when she said, 'He is over at Jacob Tall Tree's home. Probably mooning after his wife.'

'I will go there. He will want to know that Black Ted Allen is here.'

'What did you say?'

The voice emanated from within, and as the door opened wider, Hawkfeather saw Dan Bliss hurrying towards him. 'Say that again.'

'I saw Black Ted Allen ride into town not long ago. He and his men are at the trading post.'

'You are sure it was him?'

'I am sure. There were three others with him.'

'Christ,' Bliss cursed. 'Tell Henry that he's to organize all the help he can in a hurry. We'll trap them before they get out of here.'

Hawkfeather nodded. 'I will go.'

The Choctaw disappeared, and Bliss said to Nita, 'I need my guns.'

'You are still not well, Dan Bliss,' Nita told him defiantly. 'You should still be in bed.'

'Damn it, woman. Don't you go ordering me around. Your man needs all the help he can get if it's Allen and his gang.'

Minutes later, Bliss was ready to go. His holster was strapped on and Nita had given him a sawn-off shotgun that her husband kept hidden away just in case of emergency. When he walked out the door, Nita murmured to herself, 'Be careful, Dan Bliss. I have a feeling that this will not go well.'

By the time he hit the street, Henry had appeared along with Jacob Tall Tree, and two other men. The Choctaw policeman said to him, 'It seems you have brought bad luck with you, Marshal. This is the second time we'll be involved in a gunfight since you arrived. Normally the only time a gun goes off around here is when my wife gets angry with me.'

'You assume that there will be gunplay, Henry?'

'You think that Ted Allen and his friends will just throw up their hands and surrender?'

'Not in this lifetime. Are these all the men you could get?'

Henry nodded.

'Damn it. I guess it'll have to do. If we get the drop on them, then it should be fine. Come on.'

The new trading post was in the centre of town, which wasn't good in the current situation. Once the shooting started, and it would start, stray bullets would fly in all directions, thus it was highly likely they would hit innocents. But if Bliss and the others waited for them to get out of town, they would lose their element of surprise.

They spread out, moving to take cover behind a water trough, some barrels, and a high-sided wagon. Five of them against four. The thing was, they were four hardened killers, used to fighting gun battles. Not like the men Henry had with him. Sure, thought Bliss, he could rely on the Choctaw policeman, but the others might just turn tail and run once the lead started to fly. He leaned against the bed of the wagon, speaking in a low voice, 'Damn it, Amos, I wish you were here.'

'Something's wrong,' Bodie whispered in Allen's ear as the Indian behind the counter filled their order.

'What is?'

'Have a look for yourself. Outside.'

Allen sighed heavily, walked over to the window, and peered out. He looked left, and then right. Then he repeated it. The street was more or less clear. 'Christ. They damn well know we're here.'

The outlaw boss pulled his six-gun and said to Henshaw, 'Get the supplies. Bring the Indian with you. We'll use him if we have to.'

The man behind the counter tried to back away, but Henshaw struck him with an open hand and then poked the barrel of his gun up under the frightened trader's chin. 'Move.'

They emerged out on to the boardwalk, their guns drawn, the fearful trader out in front of them.

Across the street, Bliss cursed beneath his breath as he watched. Somehow, they'd gotten wind of it. Bliss straightened up. 'Hold it there, Allen. We've got you in our sights.'

'Hell almighty,' Allen cursed out loud. 'Is that you, Bliss?'

'It is.'

'Try anything and the Injun gets a bullet in the back of his head.'

'We'll still get you,' Bliss pointed out.

'Maybe so. But I'm willing to take that risk. I ain't going back to Fort Smith with you. Not for that buzzard Parker to hang me.'

They started to move closer to where their horses were tied, out on the street.

'Last chance, Allen,' Bliss shouted.

'You go to hell, Bliss!'

Allen brought up his six-gun and snapped off a shot at the deputy. The bullet cracked close to Bliss' head which made him duck. The deputy swore vehemently and fired two of his own shots at the outlaws.

One of the bullets hit the Swede in the shoulder. Crying out, the injured man tried to bring his own gun into play. By now Henry and the others were firing, and it was inevitable that a stray slug would hit the trader. It was only a matter of time. So, Bliss beat it to the punch.

While Allen had taken cover behind the trader's form and was firing from there, certain that they would not risk killing their own, Bliss sighted along the barrel of his six-gun and shot the frightened man in the leg.

He cried out and dropped like a stone when the limb gave way beneath him. Fully exposed now, Allen swore at Bliss and then shouted to his men, 'Get mounted!'

Trying to dodge the bullets coming for them, they scrambled for their horses and into the saddles. The big Swede was struggling with his wound and only just managed to get astride his bay. Even when he did, he didn't stay there for long. Slugs hammered into his chest and Eriksonn threw up his arms, falling hard to the ground. Allen's prancing mount dropped a hoof on to his chest and Bliss could all but feel the ribs give under the weight of beast and rider.

Henshaw was the first of the outlaws to break free of the death trap. He spurred his horse hard and it

103

lunged into a run. Behind him, Bodie did the same, but his horse stumbled, righted itself, and then broke into a gallop.

Allen, however, wasn't as lucky. His horse caught a stray bullet and it went down, throwing its rider forwards, sending the outlaw sprawling on to the street. He hit his head hard, and stars flashed before his eyes. His blurred vision prevented him from focusing, and by the time he was able to, he was staring into the muzzle of Dan Bliss's six-gun.

The deputy gave him a cold smile and said, 'Move and you're dead, you son-of-a-bitch.'

Devlin's Peak, Arkansas

It was after midday when Faraday began to worry about Saracen. He'd been back and forth along the street twice, but still couldn't find him. Now, with the rain settling in, he was getting more than a little wet. He saw Merriweather on the boardwalk across the street. Heading in that direction, he stomped through the mud and up the steps, and asked, 'Have you seen Saracen anywhere?'

Merriweather stared at him before shaking his head. 'Not since earlier.'

'When was that?'

'A few hours now.'

'Did he say what he was going to do, at all?'

'No. He just asked me where he might find Drake Belden, and then he left.'

'What did you tell him?' Faraday asked impatiently.

'I told him about the sawmill that Belden owns.'

Faraday thought for a moment, and something told him that Saracen had done something stupid and gone off on his own. 'Where is it?'

Merriweather told him.

'Thanks,' Faraday said and ran off to the jail. He'd need his rifle.

Ten minutes later he had a saddled horse hired from the livery. He was just about to lead it out when four horses thundered past in a spray of mud and water. Faraday cursed when he saw who it was. Looked like trouble. Why else would Craig Belden be leading three others out of town? Two of which were his hired guns.

Saracen was indeed in trouble.

Choctaw Nation

Bodie and Henshaw reined in when they figured they were safe from pursuit. They had travelled approximately six miles from Anson's Post. Bodie turned his horse to look for signs that they were being followed. The horses snorted, their sides lathered from the furious ride.

'Christ, what was that?' Henshaw blurted out. 'What happened to Ted?'

'His horse got hit and fell,' Bodie said, his voice grim.

'We gotta go back and get him,' Henshaw stated.

Bodie looked at him in disbelief. 'Are you crazy? We can't go back in there. They'd shoot us down before we got halfway along the street.'

'Well, what are we going to do?' Henshaw demanded.

'We'll need help. We'll find Cramer. Get him to help us.'

'What about the damned train with the shipment on it?'

'There'll be more.'

The baby-faced outlaw shook his head and then swore.

'What?' Bodie asked.

'The money from the last bank we robbed was on Ted's horse.'

Fort Smith, Arkansas

'. . . and so, being found guilty by a jury of your peers for the crime of murder, Simon Field, I hereby sentence you to be hanged by the neck until you are dead.'

A murmur of approval rippled through the packed gallery at the judgment.

'No!' the defendant bleated. 'No, Judge. I didn't mean it. It just happened. It was an accident.'

Parker banged the gavel down and said in a raised voice. 'Get him out of here. Next case.'

Field was dragged by two marshals from the courthouse, and placed back in the cells beneath the building, to begin his final wait to meet the hangman. It was a common occurrence. They came in all quiet and left making a big fuss.

The next case was against a young man accused of stealing a horse whilst he was drunk. Parker knew, without a doubt, he was guilty, and it seemed a shame that one night of drunken foolishness was about to cost him a year in the pen.

As the defendant was led in, with the trial about to get underway, Bass Reeves entered the courthouse. He caught Parker's eye, holding up a piece of paper for him to see. The judge waved him forward and Reeves hurried to the bench.

'What is it?' Parker growled.

'Sorry, Judge. I figured you'd want to see this.'

'Give it here.'

Reeves passed the paper over and Parker scanned it. His eyes darted back to his marshal and he asked, 'Is this for real?'

'Yes, sir.'

Isaac Parker came to his feet and took up his gavel again. He banged it so hard that it seemed likely to break, as he'd done on numerous occasions before. Then he spoke at the top of his voice, 'Court is adjourned until tomorrow. Clear the room. Mr Clayton, please remain behind. Marshal Reeves, you and Marshal Murray too.'

Once the court was vacated, Parker came down from the bench and passed the note to Clayton. 'Good news, William. It seems that the bastard killer, Black Ted Allen, has fallen into our laps. The message is from Dan Bliss. It seems that while he was recovering at Anson's, Allen and his men rode in. With help from some of the locals, one of the gang was killed and Allen captured.'

'That is good news,' Murray said.

Parker nodded. 'Indeed. I want you to take some men and a wagon and head on over there. Bring that black-hearted bastard back here for hanging.'

'I'll see to it right away.'

Murray left the courtroom and was followed outside by Reeves who stopped him on the steps. 'Be careful, Murray. You know what Allen is like. Slippery as a fish fresh from the water. You think you have him, and then with one flick of its tail, the damned thing is gone.'

'You worry too much, Bass,' Murray tried to reassure his friend.

Arkansas

Faraday was starting to feel the chill of being wet for too long. He'd been following Belden and the others through a constant curtain of rain which hadn't eased until he'd pulled off the trail on the ridge where Saracen had gone earlier in the day.

From a short distance into the trees, he watched them ride into the sawmill. They drew their horses to a halt near one of three large log cabins and went inside.

The deputy dismounted and edged forwards to the treeline. He could hear nothing but the sound of water dripping from the branches and leaves above him. Some fell with loud splats on the brim of his hat.

Behind the sawmill, the ridges were shrouded in moisture-laden clouds, and a drab grey mist drifted further down the slopes.

For ten minutes he waited, observing the scene to see what would happen. Then he saw Belden emerge through the doorway, accompanied by the men he'd ridden in with. They mounted their horses and started back towards town. Faraday eased his way away from the edge and retreated into the trees where his horse was tied to a branch. He placed his hand over its muzzle to keep it quiet.

The party of riders galloped past his position, up the slope, and over the crest. The deputy released his horse and walked to the edge of the trees again. He watched and waited. Then he saw them.

From the cabin emerged three men – and Saracen!

They took him across to where his horse was tied but walked past it. They disappeared beyond the mill area and into the stand of trees behind it. Faraday knew that their actions could mean only one thing. They were taking Saracen to kill him.

'Your pa just rode in, Drake,' Butler said.

'Good. Maybe we can get this over and done, now,' Drake sneered.

Saracen kept his face passive. Things were beyond grim, but he wasn't about to let them see it.

Drake gloated at him, 'Get ready to die, lawman. It won't be long now. I might even pull the trigger myself.'

Saracen set his jaw firm. He said, 'Do you want me facing away from you when you do it?'

Drake snarled and lashed out with an open hand. It cracked against the ex-scout's cheek, who tasted blood immediately. Saracen's rock-hard fist shot out, mashing Drake's lips and teeth together, causing him to reel back and crash to the floor.

The younger Belden lay stunned for a moment while two of the timbermen grabbed hold of Saracen.

Shaking his head to clear his vision, Drake snarled after wiping the blood from his split lips. He came to his feet and drew his six-gun. He was about to kill Saracen when a loud voice stopped him cold.

'Hold it there, boy!' Craig Belden snapped.

'I'm going to kill him, Pa. Right now.'

'Not here,' his gaze fixed on Saracen. 'So, you didn't take my advice.'

Every man with Craig Belden was soaked through and covered in mud. Saracen held his stare. 'Let's just say I don't like murderers who kill women.'

'The girl was a whore who led my boy astray.'

'Pa!' Drake protested.

'It's true. You were fine before you met her. If you ask me, her death was best for everyone.'

'Only a son-of-a-bitch like you would think that way,' Saracen growled. 'Your son won't get away with it. There'll be more marshals.'

'Maybe. But they won't find you or your friend.'

Saracen's blood ran cold. 'You've killed him?'

'Not yet. But we can't kill you and leave him running around, can we?'

Saracen struggled to break loose from the two men holding him. Trouble was, they swung axes for a living and had the strength to prove it. He was held fast.

Craig Belden shook his head. 'I've had enough. Take him out into the forest and put a bullet in his head. Leave him for the critters.'

'I'll do it,' Drake Belden said hurriedly.

110

His father stared at him in silence before saying, 'Fine. Be back in town tomorrow. We'll have the other tidied up by then.'

Saracen saw Smith give a nod to Joe Bond who then said, 'I'll give him a hand, Mr Belden. Make sure it's done right.'

'No,' the older Belden snapped. 'It's time the boy learned to stand on his own two feet. He killed the girl with no problems. Let's see if he can do it to a man.'

The challenge was out there for all to see and Drake glared at his father with open hostility. 'Are you saying I'm yeller, Pa?'

'I'm saying, don't mess it up.'

CHAPTER 8

Arkansas

The rain seemed to be heavier still, if that were possible. Skirting the sawmill with his horse, Faraday followed the party back into the trees. After three hundred yards or so, he dismounted, slipped his Winchester from the saddle scabbard, and now pursued them on foot.

The group stopped around five hundred yards from the mill. They stood swapping words in the tree-filtered rain for almost a minute, and then one of them raised a six-gun to shoot Saracen.

The move surprised Faraday even though he was expecting it. He snapped off a shot with the Winchester, and the would-be shooter yelped in pain and dropped the weapon in his hand, staggering backwards.

Saracen reacted instantly, lunging to scoop up the fallen six-gun. The other pair scrabbled frantically to bring their weapons to bear in Faraday's direction.

Firing again, the Winchester's bark whiplashed through the forest. The slug caught Butler in the chest and he slumped to the ground. Directly after the last man fired in the direction of the unseen threat, Saracen shot him with his newly acquired weapon.

The bullet from the six-gun ripped through the timber-cutter's throat in a spray of crimson. Clutching at the ghastly wound, the big man fell to the wet ground, trembling violently as he bled out, his life source mixing with muddy water to form a rusty puddle.

Saracen immediately swivelled round to bring the six-gun to cover the writhing form of Drake Belden on the saturated ground.

As the echoes of the gunfire dissipated, Faraday emerged from the trees. He didn't look happy at all.

'You're a damned fool, Saracen. Why do you think you have a partner?'

'I know. What I did was stupid. I'm sorry.'

'Yeah, well, you won't do it again. You were just lucky I figured it out.'

'Thank you,' Saracen said and then asked, 'What are we going to do with our wounded friend?'

'Take him back.'

'To Devlin's Peak? We sure can't go back there. Craig Belden and the others were going back after you.'

Faraday nodded. He pointed to Drake. 'We'd best get him on a horse then. Yours is back at the mill. We'll get everything we need and then head back to Fort Smith. With a little luck, we'll get a good jump on them. We can come back for the others later.'

'Won't have to. They'll come after us, for sure.'

'Then we'll have to kill them.'

Saracen leaned down, checking the younger Belden over. The bullet from Faraday's Winchester had blown a walnut-sized hole in his upper thigh. His leg was bleeding, but the bullet had passed through.

Saracen grabbed him by the collar and dragged him to his feet.

'Ahhhh!' he protested, yowling with pain. 'Take it easy. I'm wounded, damn it.'

The ex-scout slapped him up the back of his head. 'Shut up.'

'You can't do that.'

He hit him again. 'I just did, now move.'

When they emerged from the forest at the back of the sawmill the rain had finally stopped. Men came from the cabins, milling about expectantly, and Faraday sighed. 'This isn't good. We're outnumbered.'

'They don't have guns, though,' Saracen pointed out.

One of the loggers stepped forward to block their path. In his right hand was a double-edged axe. 'Where do you think you're going?'

Faraday said, 'Do you want to handle this, or shall I?'

'I'll take care of it,' Saracen said, shooting the man in the leg with the six-gun in his fist.

The logger fell into the mud at his feet with a screech of pain. The ex-scout shifted his aim and called out, 'If the rest of you fellers don't want to stop lead, then I suggest you stay right where you are.'

No one moved.

'Do you all have another horse somewhere?' Faraday asked.

One of the men nodded.

'Get it.'

Once he was gone, Saracen said to the others, 'Everyone drop your weapons and get back inside the cabin.'

After they were ushered inside, Saracen found his Schofield and holster, along with his Winchester.

The man who'd gone for the horse, returned with a fully saddled bay. Faraday locked him up with the others while Saracen got Drake on to the horse.

'You're going to have to help me on, the way this leg of mine is,' he whined.

'Get on yourself or walk.'

'At least we should be quicker without the wagon,' Faraday told Saracen. 'Although the judge won't like it. Costs money, he'll say.'

'Well, if we have to come back to get Belden, then at least it'll still be in town.'

'Yeah, if. Let's get out of here.'

Ten minutes later they were ready to ride.

Devlin's Peak

It took the loggers an hour to escape from the cabin and get into town to inform Craig Belden of what had happened to his son. Needless to say he was far from happy.

'And you useless bastards let them take my son? Christ, what the hell do I pay you for?' he stormed.

'We ain't gunmen,' the logger said. 'Our business is trees.'

115

'Your business is whatever I tell you to do, damn it! Get out.'

The red-faced man left the room and Belden whirled on Smith and Bond. 'Find some men. And by men, I mean men. I don't want a bunch of them with a mile-wide yellow streak down their backs. We ride in an hour.'

Ouachita Mountains, Arkansas

'We're being followed,' Saracen told Faraday.

'How do you know?' the deputy asked.

'I saw their fire while I was taking a piss. They're across the valley.'

They'd pushed hard for the remainder of the day, and after crossing the narrow valley, had found a bench where they could set up camp. The younger Belden had moaned all the way, and at one point Saracen had seriously considered knocking him out just for some peace and quiet.

'He'll kill you when he catches up,' Drake sneered.

'Shut your hole,' Faraday snapped from his position next to the small campfire, 'or I'll shut it for you.'

'Go to hell.'

Faraday came to his feet with a snarl.

'Amos!' Saracen barked.

The deputy glared at the smiling Drake and sat back down. Saracen picked up his Winchester and said, 'Keep an eye on him. I'll be back before morning.'

A worried expression came across Faraday's face. 'Where are you going?'

'They can't do much without horses.'

'You're going back there.'

Saracen nodded.

'I don't like it. Let's just keep going. Tonight.'

The ex-scout shook his head. 'We can't. Just before we made camp my horse picked up a stone bruise. He needs rest.'

'Damn it.'

'I'll be back. I'll steal one of their horses while I'm at it.'

'Are you sure you can do it?'

Saracen smiled. 'I stayed alive scouting Apaches. These fellers ain't got nothing on them.'

'Well, good luck then.'

'If I ain't back come morning, keep going. Just leave my horse here in case I need it.'

Faraday looked confused. 'But you said he was lame.'

Saracen nodded. 'He is.'

It took Saracen three hours by foot through the chill of the night to reach the pursuers' camp. At least the rain had stopped, which made his journey less miserable. When he reached it, however, he found only one man on watch, or supposedly on watch. Instead, Saracen crept past the sleeping man, which was just an open invitation to an intruder to cut his throat.

Moving in silence around the camp, he reached the horse picket. One by one he unhitched all eight of them, keeping hold of the last one for himself. He was about to mount up when a disturbance from the camp drew his attention. Then came loud voices.

'You stupid son of a bitch,' the voice snarled. 'What the hell are you doing? Asleep on watch. I ought to put a damned bullet in you right now.'

'What's going on?' another voice called out. Saracen recognized it as Craig Belden's.

'This asshole went to sleep on watch.'

More voices.

Saracen didn't like it. Too much activity. He started to mount the bay he'd chosen when a shout reached his ears.

'The horses! Someone is at the horses!'

The ex-scout wrapped his left hand in the horse's mane and swung himself up on to it bareback. He kept the reins and the Winchester in his left hand, and with his right, pulled the Schofield. He fired twice into the air and shouted 'Heyaa!'

The horses started to bolt into the darkness as bullets from Belden's men cut the air about Saracen's head. He fired back and heard one of them cry out. Then he kicked the bay hard and it leaped forwards.

More gunfire crashed out, but it was all in vain because Saracen was gone.

Choctaw Nation

Bodie and Henshaw found Cramer and his gang early the next morning. The outlaws were waiting on the Shoestring River. Cramer, a short man at a shade over five and a half feet, had a reputation that always made him seem bigger.

He rode with four followers: Larry Kane, Ben

Wilson, Rat Finch and a Cherokee Indian only referred to as the Renegade.

'Where's Allen?' Cramer growled when they arrived.

'He got caught over in Anson's,' Bodie explained.

'Damn it!' the outlaw exclaimed. 'We're meant to hit that blasted train together.'

'If you can get him out, he might have an idea about something else.'

'I should let the bastard hang, is what I should do. What was he doing in Anson's, anyway?'

'We were getting supplies,' Bodie told him the rest as he looked around the camp.

Cramer noticed, and said, 'She ain't here.'

'What?'

'The woman. I got rid of her.'

'You killed her?' Bodie blurted out.

'No. I sold her to a trader up in Kansas.'

'Oh.'

Cramer stared at him with suspicion. 'What were you saying about something else?'

'Ted happened to mention a bank or some such that had a big shipment of gold passing through it,' Bodie lied. 'He was thinking about making a try for it after the train.'

The outlaw boss's eyes narrowed. 'Where?'

'He didn't say.'

'The marshals would have received word by now. They'll have men coming to pick him up for trial.'

'Then we'd best hurry.'

'Yeah. We'd best.'

Anson's Post

'Are you sure you're right to come with us, Dan?' Murray asked Bliss.

'Just try and stop me,' Bliss growled. 'I want to see this son-of-a-bitch hang.'

Murray and four other marshals had ridden into Anson's the evening before, after pushing hard, even with the wagon.

'You ain't got me there yet, lawdogs,' Allen snarled from behind the bars of the tumbleweed wagon.

'Shut your yap, Allen,' Bliss snapped. 'And keep it shut all the way back to Fort Smith.'

'You know what, Marshal?' Allen said.

'What?'

'I'm going to enjoy killing you.'

Murray said, 'Watch your mouth, Allen. You might just not make it back to hang.'

The outlaw snorted but remained silent.

Bliss said to Murray, 'How come Amos ain't with you?'

'He's over in Devlin's Peak with the new feller.'

'What new feller?'

'That feller you two hooked up with. Saracen.'

'He stayed on?' Bliss said in wonderment. 'I thought he would have moved on, looking for his sister.'

Bliss fixed his steely gaze on the outlaw. He'd asked Allen about Saracen's sister, but the outlaw remained tight-lipped.

'Saracen didn't have much choice. The judge threatened to lock him up if he didn't go with Amos.'

'What?'

'I'll tell you along the trail.'

Henry Grey Elk stood off to the side and watched the marshals get organized. Nita joined him, and Bliss walked across to them. He took her by the hand and said, 'Thanks for taking care of me, Nita.'

She smiled at him. 'It was no trouble, Dan Bliss. You come back and visit whenever you wish.'

'If it means getting more of your cooking, I'll definitely be back.'

She gave a warm laugh.

He shifted his gaze to Henry and held out his hand. 'Thanks, Henry.'

'Be careful of this one, Dan Bliss. He is like the serpent.'

Bliss could see the concern in his eyes. 'Take more than a snake to bring me down, Henry.'

Henry grunted.

Bliss climbed on to his horse and joined Murray and the other marshals.

'You ready?' Murray asked.

'Yeah. Let's get this son-of-a-bitch out of here.'

Choctaw Nation

'Parker set him up like that?' Bliss asked in disbelief.

Murray nodded. 'Yep.'

'I always knew he was a wily bastard, but I never thought he'd do something like that.'

Picking their way along the rutted trail, the horses

led the way for the tumbleweed wagon which lurched into a deep rut then out the other side. A muffled curse emanated from within when Allen whacked his head on one of the bars.

Murray said, 'I heard tell that Allen took Saracen's sister. Killed his parents, too.'

'Yeah.'

'Did you ask him about the woman?'

'Sure did. Son-of-a-bitch didn't say a word. I reckon he or one of his gang killed her.'

Murray sighed. 'More than likely.'

Bliss said, 'I'm sure of one thing. When Saracen sees him, I'd hate to be in his boots.'

They rode on in silence, each deep in their own thoughts. Soon after midday, they stopped by a narrow, slow-moving stream. They watered the horses and took a break in the shade of some large oaks.

Allen was permitted to stretch his legs briefly, under their watchful eyes, before being returned to his secure mode of transportation, and they were under-way again less than an hour after stopping.

The condition of the trail grew worse ahead, and they were forced to slow even more. One of the stream crossings was higher than normal and it took a while to get the wagon across.

'Do you think anyone would miss him if he drowned?' Murphy asked Bliss, seeing the swirling water begin lapping at the wagon bed.

'I know I wouldn't.'

The wagon lurched over one last large rock as it emerged from the stream in a cascade of water. Two riders followed it out on to the bank. On a hill to the north of them, a lone horseman at the edge of a stand of trees was missed by every one of the marshals.

The Renegade rode a strong-looking buckskin into Cramer's makeshift camp an hour later. His hawkish features were set in a grim expression. He dismounted and walked over to the group.

'Well?' asked Cramer.

The Cherokee grunted. 'I found them.'

'Where?'

He told them about the wagon crossing the stream. 'If we leave now we can catch them when they cross the Snake Creek.'

'Let's ride, then,' Henshaw stated as he climbed to his feet.

'Just hold up there, young feller,' Cramer cautioned.

'What?'

'These are my men. I give the orders.'

'Well, then, give them,' Bodie snapped.

The outlaw glared at him. 'Watch yourself. Remember who you're talking to.'

Bodie bit back a retort and Cramer looked at the others. 'Get your horses.' He turned his attention back to Bodie. A cold glint entered his eyes. 'And if you ever speak to me like that again, I'll plant you. Now get the hell on your horse.'

CHAPTER 9

Fort Smith, Arkansas

'We made it,' Faraday voiced his observation as they rode along the street towards the courthouse. 'You figure they'll come into town?'

Saracen wasn't sure, but something told him that Craig Belden wasn't one to give up without a fight. 'Maybe.'

'He'll come,' Drake snarled. 'And when he does, he'll kill both of you and anyone who gets in his way.'

'I wouldn't,' Saracen said.

'Wouldn't what?'

'Come after a son-of-a-bitch like you. But I guess you and him are cut from the same bolt of cloth.'

They rode up to the courthouse and Faraday dragged Drake from the saddle. The killer protested his rough treatment, but the deputy ignored him.

'Go easy, damn it. I need to see a doctor.'

'You hear something like a whining sound, Blaine?' Faraday asked.

'Nope.'

'Me neither.'

Bass Reeves appeared on the steps and stared down at the men. 'Where's the wagon?'

'Had to leave it behind,' Faraday told him.

'Judge ain't going to like that. Them things cost money. Judge hates to lose money.'

They helped Drake up the steps.

'What happened to his leg?'

'I fell over and bit it,' Drake snarled. 'What the hell do you think happened, you idiot?'

Reeves' fist travelled less than a foot before crashing into Drake's guts, doubling him over. Air whooshed from his lungs and he gagged.

'Mouthy son-of-a-bitch, ain't he?' Bass observed.

Saracen nodded. 'You could say that.'

The sound of hoofs reached their ears and the three lawmen turned to see Craig Belden and five other men riding hard along the street. Townsfolk scattered as the riders thundered by.

'Got here quicker than I figured,' Faraday said.

Saracen grunted. 'Yeah.'

'Who are they?' Reeves asked.

'Craig Belden and his hired thugs,' Saracen told him. 'We had some trouble with them.'

'Looks like you're about to have some more.'

Saracen cocked the hammer on his Winchester and held it across his body. Faraday rested his hand on his six-gun and noted that Reeves wasn't wearing one.

'You missing something, Bass?'

'In court today, Amos. You know the judge don't like guns inside.'

The riders stopped ten or so yards from the court-house and fanned out in a line with Craig Belden at their centre. Either side of him were his thugs, Smith and Bond, plus the others.

'Let my boy go, Saracen!' Craig Belden demanded.

'You want to come up here and take his place?' the former scout asked.

The older Belden snorted. 'Let him go, and we won't kill you.'

The man had guts, had to give him that. Riding into a town full of United States marshals to get his son back took some doing. 'Sorry, Craig. Can't do that. I can do this though. You're under arrest. Throw down your guns.'

Craig Belden's eyes narrowed. His voice was a hiss. 'If you think you can.'

Saracen said, 'Bass, you might want to step away.'

Of course it made sense, but the deputy didn't move. Instead he said, 'I'm good right here.'

Faraday said, 'You just court trouble, don't you, Saracen?'

There was a drawn-out silence before Bond moved. His hand blurred and came up filled with his six-gun. Saracen brought the Winchester around and fired from the hip. Narrowly missing the head of Bond's horse, the slug smashed into its rider's chest.

The horse reared and tipped the mortally wounded killer from the saddle. He landed in a tangle of arms and legs beneath the animal's hoofs.

Beside Saracen, Faraday had brought up his own six-gun and snapped off a shot at one of Craig

126

Belden's hired guns, the slug burying deep in the muscle of the man's shoulder, rocking him in the saddle.

Smith had a weapon out and fired a shot at Saracen, who felt the hot wind of its passing close to his face.

Saracen levered and fired twice at the killer. The first bullet missed, but the second tore a ghastly wound in the man's throat, spraying blood across Craig Belden's face.

More shots sounded, and when the gunfire ceased, Craig Belden was the only one of the riders still on his horse. His face was as white as a sheet.

'What have I done?' he murmured.

Saracen thought that he was the subject of the man's comment. Then he realized that he was looking past him. He turned to see Drake Belden on the steps, bleeding from at least two wounds, dead.

Saracen glanced about and saw that both Faraday and Reeves were all right.

There was movement behind them as figures emerged from the courthouse.

'What in damnation is going on here?' a gruff voice growled.

Saracen stared at Isaac Parker. 'Just bringing in your prisoner, Judge.'

'Damn well interrupting my court is what you're doing. A man should lock you lot up for disturbing the peace is what he should do. Shit, I think I might at that.'

'Just ease your wagon a mite, Judge,' Reeves said. 'It ain't their fault.'

'Well, somebody sure as shit shot these fellers, Bass,' Parker snapped. 'Or did they do it themselves?'

Saracen stared at Parker and shook his head. 'Maybe I should have let them shoot me instead. Might have been a sight easier than dealing with a coot like you.'

'Watch your mouth, *Deputy* Saracen,' the judge growled.

The former scout's eyes flared, and his mouth opened to fire back a rebuke. But Faraday's voice cut across him: 'God damn it, Judge. We ain't had no choice in the matter. Ever since we left here we had fellers trying to kill us. We reached Devlin's Peak and found the sheriff hanging by his neck. We had all kinds of trouble getting our prisoner back. Then when we do, his pa rides into town with his hired guns and tries to kill us. And on top of that, you bawl us out for doing our job. I'm seriously thinking that the next time you want something done, to tell you to do the blamed thing yourself.'

Behind Parker stood a small group of marshals, each one with a broad smile on his face. Parker turned, and they melted into the crowd in a flash. He turned back and ran his gaze over Faraday and Saracen. Giving a jerky nod, he said, 'Come and see me after court. I'll get a full report then.'

The judge turned and walked back inside. Reeves slapped Faraday on his back and laughed. 'I guess you sure told him, Amos.'

'I hate being told how to do my job. Besides, I'd just been shot at. Kinda puts a man on edge.'

'What'll we do about him?' Saracen asked, indicating Craig Belden.

'I'll take care of him,' Bass said. 'You fellers go and get cleaned up. I'll see you later for a beer. I've something to tell you.'

Saracen was curious. 'What?'

Reeves thought about delaying it, then decided against it. 'We caught Black Ted Allen.'

'What?'

'He showed up at Anson's. Dan Bliss and some of the Lighthorse took him prisoner. They're on their way back here.'

Saracen grabbed Reeves by the arm. 'Is she with them? Is Vicki with them?'

'I don't know. No one said.'

'I gotta get out there and meet them.'

'Ease up, hoss. They'll be back in Fort Smith tomorrow. Leave it until then. It ain't long to wait.'

'He's right, Saracen,' Amos agreed.

Saracen nodded. 'All right, I'll wait. But if she ain't with them, I'll kill him.'

'I have your towels and more hot water, Marshal Saracen,' Molly called out, and then opened the door to the bathroom.

There was a splash of water and soap as Saracen tried to cover himself. 'Whoa, ma'am. What are you doing?'

She waved a hand at him. 'Don't be such a fuddy-duddy. I'm a much travelled woman. I've seen what most men have to offer.'

'You ain't seen what I have to offer, ma'am.'

She placed the towels on a chair and paused. 'You're right about that.'

She walked across to the tub and poured the water in. Once she was finished she placed the jug down and her eyes flashed. She gave him a coy smile. Her right index finger traced its way across one of his broad shoulders. With her other hand, she undid the strings at the top of her dress to reveal the white tops of her breasts. 'How about you show me?'

Saracen smiled at her brazenness. 'Sorry, ma'am. I'm all in. I've been riding a horse all day, with fellers chasing me to boot.'

Her hand ran across his muscular chest and twirled through the thick hair it encountered. 'If it's a horse you want, I'm game. I've been a lot of things.'

Saracen reached up and removed her hand before it could go any further. 'I'm fine thanks, ma'am. Maybe another time.'

She straightened and tied her dress strings. 'Oh, well. Can't blame a girl for trying.'

He breathed a sigh of relief when she left, and took the opportunity to stand up in the tub and let the excess water drain from his body. Then he climbed out and reached for a towel.

There was a faint noise from the door and he glanced in its direction. He frowned, then smiled knowingly. The keyhole.

Saracen crossed to the door and placed the towel on the knob so that it draped across the hole. He smiled again.

On the other side, Molly straightened and pulled a face. Then she, too, smiled. She enjoyed a challenge, and Blaine Saracen was shaping up as the biggest challenge she'd had in a long time.

Choctaw Territory

The last thing on Dan Bliss's mind as they approached Snake Creek was an ambush. His newly healed wound had started hurting like a bitch five miles back, and the pain had made him weary and angry.

'Where are we going to damned well camp, Murray?' Bliss growled. 'I got me a burr under my saddle that only a good night's sleep will fix.'

'How about we set up on the other side of the Snake?' Murray proposed.

'Damned fine idea.'

'I'll set the others on watch tonight so you can sleep through, Dan. That wound of yours giving you what for?'

Bliss grunted. 'Yeah. I thought it would be good. Obviously getting shot takes more out of a feller than what I realized.'

'Won't be long now and we'll be stopped.'

'Yeah.'

The wagon rattled along behind them, squeaking and lurching every time it hit a rut or rock in the trail. Inside, Allen rocked and rolled with the motion until finally, the Snake came into view.

'Made it,' Murray said.

They led the wagon down the bank and into the water. It was slow flowing and came up to the horse's girths. The wagon rolled down the slope and splashed into the water. The horses strained against the traces from the extra resistance created by the water.

They were halfway across when Bliss drew back on the reins of his horse. 'Christ, no!'

'What is it?' Murray asked as he did the same.

Behind them, there was a curse as the wagon driver followed suit along with the other riders.

Bliss screwed up his face. 'There's someone in the trees on the other side.'

'What?' Murray asked, confused, and as he did so, rose in the stirrups to get a better look.

A rifle shot crashed out and the slug slammed into Murray's chest. The deputy toppled sideways, landing in the creek with a loud splash. That was the signal for the rest of the bushwhackers to open fire.

The far bank pulsed to life as a blanket of gunfire erupted. Behind Bliss, the wagon driver cried out, his chest a mass of red. Another rider fell from the saddle while he was trying to extract his carbine from its scabbard.

Bliss pulled his six-gun and fired wildly in the direction of the hidden shooters while trying to get his horse turned. Feeling the burn of a bullet low down in his back, he hissed with the pain. Biting back a curse, he drove his heels into the horse's flanks and it lunged forwards, sending a spray of water before its powerful body.

As he levered a fresh round into his Winchester, he saw another marshal fall from the saddle.

'Get back!' Bliss shouted to the remaining men.

'For Chris'sakes, get back!'

Another went down, which left only a wounded Bliss and one other.

A second bullet hammered into Bliss's back. This one hurt more than the last one and he knew he'd been hit hard. He felt his strength begin to wane and lost his grip on the six-gun in his fist.

A shout of pain to his right told Bliss that the last deputy was down, and judging by the way he felt, he knew he wasn't far behind. Bliss cursed out loud just before the final bullet punched into the back of his head, killing him.

An eerie silence descended over the Snake. The last echoes of gunfire rolled away into oblivion. Then the hush was pierced by an almost maniacal laugh.

Slowly, men emerged from the trees and stood on the bank. Bodie called out, 'You OK, Ted?'

The laughing stopped. 'That you, Bodie?'

'Sure is.'

'Who you got with you?'

'Cramer.'

'No shit?'

'Yeah, it's me, Ted,' Cramer called.

'Didn't figure I'd see you.'

'I told him about the gold shipment going through that bank you was telling us about.'

Allen frowned. 'Really?'

'Yeah, really.'

The outlaw thought for a moment and shouted back. 'All right. The more the merrier. What there is will go around. Now, how about getting me out of here.'

133

Ten minutes later they had the tumbleweed wagon on the far bank and Allen was pleased to be free of his confinement. The outlaws were all gathered around him. Allen stared at Henshaw and said, 'Give me your gun.'

Not wanting to argue with his boss, Henshaw did as ordered.

'So, what's this gold shipment your man was telling me about?' Cramer asked.

Allen looked the outlaw in the eyes and said, 'There ain't one.'

With that, he shot Cramer in the chest.

The outlaw was flung on to his back. By the time he hit the ground Allen had moved the six-gun to cover the rest of Cramer's men. He said, 'The way I see it, you fellers have got two choices. Join up with me or join your boss. Personally, I can use the help, so it sure would be a shame to have to shoot you.'

Kane said, 'I guess we don't have much choice.'

Allen gave him a cold smile. 'Not from where I'm standing.'

Rat Finch stared down at Cramer's body. He hawked and spit on the corpse. 'I'm in.'

'Where are we going?' asked Wilson.

'Kansas,' Allen said. 'I know a feller up there who might be able to give us some valuable information.'

Bodie smiled. 'Hey, we might see that woman.'

'What woman?'

'The one you gave to Cramer. He sold her to a trader up there.'

'Yeah, well guess what? That woman has a brother,

134

and right at this time he's looking for her. Which means he's looking for us.'

'How do you know that?'

Allen stared out into the creek and nodded at the body hung up on a snag close to the far bank. He grinned and said, 'Deputy United States Marshal Dan Bliss.'

'Well then, let's get the hell out of here,' Bodie urged his boss.

'All in good time. First, we have to make a stopover.'

'Where?'

'Anson's Post.'

'Aw, hell,' Bodie whined. 'Why would you want to go back there?'

'I owe them, that's why.'

Fort Smith, Arkansas

'Congratulations on a successful mission, Mr Saracen,' Chief Marshal Kent Hudgins said from where he was sitting in one of the judge's leather-backed chairs. 'I know this is the first time we've met, but I've heard a lot about you. Welcome aboard.'

'I ain't aboard,' Saracen told him.

He shot a questioning glance at Parker. 'Oh?'

'Saracen has a burr under his saddle about finding his sister. Ted Allen took her, but his questions should be answered soon because we finally caught the bastard.'

'We'll see,' said Saracen.

Parker sighed. 'Anyway, you need to tell us what happened at Devlin's Peak.'

Between them, they related to Parker and Hudgins everything that had happened. Parker remained silent throughout. Once they'd finished he nodded and said, 'Write out your expenses and give them to Kent. He'll sort out reimbursement.'

Saracen started to take the badge from his shirt and Parker frowned at him. 'What are you doing?'

'Giving you back this badge. I'm done.'

The judge shook his head. 'No, you ain't done. Not until I say you are.'

'That's horseshit.'

'You'll find out about your sister tomorrow when the others arrive back, and then I have another job for you and Amos.'

'Doing what?' Saracen snapped.

'Prisoner pick-up from Muskogee.'

'You're unbelievable.'

Parker glanced at Hudgins. The chief marshal said, 'At the moment, the marshals are stretched thin right across the district. It was one of the reasons I wasn't here when you first arrived. I was out running down a murderer. For some reason, all the outlaws across the west have decided to congregate in our area and I need more marshals. I can assure you that after you do this last job, you'll be able to hand your badge back. Right, Judge?'

Parker murmured something under his breath.

'Right?' Hudgins said again.

'Right.'

Saracen shook his head. 'You'll forgive me if I don't believe you.'

The chief marshal shrugged.

'Who is the feller we're going to fetch back?' Faraday asked.

'John Hawk,' Hudgins told him.

Faraday's face remained passive. 'Uh huh.'

'Who's John Hawk?' Saracen asked.

'Black Creek Lighthorseman,' Hudgins told him. 'There's been some trouble between them and the Cherokee Lighthorse of late, and he killed one. Normally they would leave it to Indian justice, but those in Muskogee want the judge to handle the trial. They figure if they do it themselves, a small war could break out between their young men.'

'And John Hawk is a Creek policeman?'

'He is.'

'This should be interesting.'

'To say the least,' agreed Hudgins.

CHAPTER 10

Fort Smith, Arkansas

Saracen waited all day for the marshals to appear with Black Ted Allen. The minutes dragged on into hours, and the day was almost gone when Faraday knocked on the door to his room.

Outside the sky held an orange glow signalling the end to the day. The marshals were supposed to have been back by noon with their prisoner. They weren't.

Faraday poked his head in the door and said, 'Hudgins wants to see us.'

'He's worried about the marshals not being back, ain't he?'

Faraday nodded. 'They should have been back a long time ago.'

'OK,' Saracen said, scooping up his Winchester from where it was leaning against a chair.

The pair hurried downstairs and out on to the street. They proceeded to the marshal's office and found Hudgins awaiting their arrival.

'I don't like it at all,' Hudgins said. 'Murray should have been back already and he ain't.'

'You want us to go and have a look?' Faraday asked.

'Yes. I was going to send Bass, but I sent him out on another job. So it seems that you two are it.'

Saracen thought for a moment. 'What do you want us to do if the worst has happened?'

'Get word back to me and continue on up to Muskogee. Pick up the prisoner John Hawk, and bring him back. I'll organize a posse of marshals to go after Allen if he's escaped. Do *not* go after him yourselves. If he has broken free, then he had help. Do you understand?'

This last was directed at Saracen, and the former scout nodded. Faraday said, 'We'll take an extra horse. Don't fancy dragging a wagon up to Muskogee.'

Hudgins waved him away. 'Whatever, Amos. Just remember what I said.'

Outside the office, Saracen asked him, 'Why don't you want to take a wagon?'

'Can't go after Allen with one of them.'

'Didn't Hudgins just finish saying not to do that?'

'Yep.'

'You think Allen's escaped.'

'Yep. Which also means if he has, he's killed every one of the men in the detail sent to get him. And if I know Dan Bliss, he was with them too. And that means he's dead along with the rest of them.'

Saracen had forgotten about Bliss. A grim expression settled on his face. 'Let's just hope they busted a wheel and got held up.'

Faraday nodded. 'Yeah. Just in case, I'll find us a pack horse and get some supplies. We could be gone a while.'

*

Saracen went back to his room and packed his saddle-bags. He found Molly and gave her some money, telling her he would be away with Amos for a while. She hurried away and came back with a small sack in her hand.

'They're biscuits,' she told him. 'Something to eat on the trail.'

'Thank you, ma'am,' he said, taking the sack.

His next stop was to get extra ammunition for the Winchester and the Schofield. He grabbed two boxes for each and then set off to find Faraday.

Amos had a bay horse packed with supplies and the other two saddle horses ready to go. It was late in the afternoon but they both figured to get some miles under their belt before dark.

'If we're ready to ride, then we may as well skedaddle on out of here,' Faraday said.

'As good a time as any,' Saracen agreed.

They rode out of Fort Smith a few minutes later, both men moving in rhythm with their horses, a pall of silence hanging over them.

Anson's Post

Henry Grey Elk knew trouble was coming well before it arrived. He could feel it. Nita looked at him across the rough table and asked, 'What is the matter?'

'Trouble.'

'What trouble?'

He shrugged and forked some more stew into his

140

mouth. 'I do not know.'

'Then how do you know trouble is coming?'

'I can feel it. It will come tonight.'

Nita sighed. 'Well, I hope we can finish our meal before it arrives.'

Henry stood up, the legs of his chair scraping on the floor. Shaking his head, he walked across to the wall pegs where his Winchester hung. He took it down and made sure it was loaded.

Nita gave him a quizzical look and he said, 'They are here.'

On cue, a horse snorted from outside. Nita's heart gave a jump.

'Are you in there, Injun?' a voice snarled.

Nita's heart jumped again, and she crossed to the window to look outside. In the last vestiges of daylight, she saw seven riders. She gasped. 'It's him, Henry. He has returned.'

'Who has returned?'

'Ted Allen.'

Henry looked at Nita then walked towards the door.

'What are you doing?' Nita asked. 'You can't go out there.'

He grunted. 'I can't stay in here, either.'

Henry Grey Elk stepped out through the doorway and stopped. He stared at Allen.

'I see that *Nanapolo* rides tonight,' he said, using the Choctaw word for evil spirit.

Allan's eyes narrowed. 'I don't know what the hell you just said, but yeah, he does.'

'It is the word my people use for men like you.

141

Where are the marshals?'

'Most of them are probably in Hell by now.'

Behind the riders a small crowd of men had begun to gather. Amongst them Henry saw Johnny Hawkfeather and Jacob Tall Tree. Both had guns with them, however, they looked troubled. And who wouldn't be, faced with a bunch of murderous killers such as these?

'I'll ask you to keep riding, Ted,' Henry said to the killer, his voice calm.

A cold smile split Allen's face. 'Ain't going to happen. This damned hole in the earth owes me and I aim to collect. Starting with your wife.'

Allen's last words were little more than a snarl. He brought up his six-gun and the killing began.

The slug from the Colt in the killer's fist slammed into Henry's chest, rocking him back on to his heels. The Choctaw policeman staggered but remained upright. With gritted teeth against the pain, Henry brought up the Winchester and squeezed the trigger.

The shot went wide of its intended target but still found flesh. Ben Wilson cried out and fell from his saddle. The bullet had caught him quite low and ripped through his guts with horrific consequence.

Allen shot the Choctaw policeman again, felling Henry with a hole through his hawkish nose.

Behind the riders, Johnny Hawkfeather and Jacob Tall Tree opened fire. Johnny's shot missed Larry Kane by a hair, but Jacob had no such problem. His bullet hammered into the side of Rat Finch who had turned in the saddle. Finch grunted and hunched over his pommel.

Lead was soon flying in all directions and many innocents were cut down in the mêlée. And while they were dying, Black Ted Allen climbed down from his saddle and walked inside the Grey Elk house.

As he entered he shouted, 'Honey, I'm home!'

Choctaw Nation

Saracen and Faraday reached Snake Creek an hour before noon the following day. They were greeted by large black buzzards who were already feasting on the bodies of the slain. The ugly creatures waddled about, gorged from their sumptuous buffet of fresh flesh.

Saracen spat and said, 'Looks like all those bad feelings we had were true.'

Faraday nodded and said, 'We'd best check them over. Poor bastards.'

They worked in silence, slowly locating all the dead. Internally, Saracen fumed at the thought of Allen getting away. At the prospect of learning nothing about his sister.

It was Faraday who found Dan Bliss. The man was still hung up on the snag where the creek had deposited him. The deputy marshal looped a rope over his friend and said, 'I'm sorry about this, Dan.'

He dragged him through the water and back to the creek bank. Once there he unlooped the rope and stared down at Bliss through tear-filled eyes, almost overwhelmed by the death of his friend. 'I'll get the bastard for you, Dan. I promise.'

There was movement near Faraday as Saracen

stepped in beside him. 'Bastards,' he muttered.

'We gotta get them buried before we go on,' Faraday said.

'Yeah, let's do it. But before we get started there's something you should see.'

Faraday followed Saracen up the bank and over a dead fall tree to a body lying on its back. The deputy stared down at the bloated corpse and said, 'Hank Cramer.'

'Who's he?'

'Outlaw. Headed up a gang of killers. I guess he helped break Allen free.'

'Thing is, now you've told me his name, do you find it odd that they bushwhacked the deputies in the creek from the other side, and yet Cramer is on this side?'

'So is the wagon,' Faraday pointed out.

'I looked at the sign. The deputies drove the wagon into the water, the outlaws ambushed it and returned to this side. If any of them were going to die, the bodies would be on the other side. I think once Cramer released Allen, he got shot for his trouble.'

Faraday nodded. 'That's a fine howdy-do.'

'The question is, why did they head back that way towards Anson's Post?'

It took the best part of two hours to bury the dead, and once they were finished, Faraday said a few words over all the graves except that of Cramer.

'What do we do with the wagon?' Saracen asked Faraday.

144

'Leave it. We need to get on the trail of these bastards.'

'I've been thinking while we were burying the others.'

'About what?' Faraday asked.

'About why Allen and the rest would head back towards Anson's.'

'And?'

'If the Choctaw police helped to capture him, then he might figure that he owes them something.'

Faraday nodded. 'You reckon he's gone back to pay them a visit because of that?'

'That would be my guess.'

'For their sakes I hope not. Because what Allen did here is only a fraction of what that bastard is capable of.'

Anson's Post

The dark smudge of smoke in the sky above Anson's Post told both men all they needed to know. It hung suspended like a filthy sheet on a giant washing line.

Saracen hauled back on the reins of his horse and Faraday did the same. The former scout said, 'That don't look too good.'

'Nope.'

Both men took out their Winchesters and urged their horses forward slowly. By the time they hit the outskirts of Anson's Post it was all too obvious what had happened. A large portion of the town had been burned. Only a few buildings had been spared, whether intentionally or not. The rest were piles of smouldering rubble. Bodies of the dead still lay in the street where they had been killed.

'It's a damned slaughter,' Faraday growled.

Saracen's face was grim, and he remained silent. They kept riding and stopped out the front of what had been Henry and Nita Grey Elk's home. Unfortunately, it mirrored the charred and smoking remains of the rest of the Post's buildings, except for one aspect. The body of Henry lay out the front where he'd been shot down.

The former scout dismounted to check on him. It was, as he'd suspected, a total waste of time. Standing up, he looked around, seeing that Faraday had dismounted too and was checking out another body.

Saracen walked over to him.

'It's Ben Wilson,' Faraday informed him. 'One of Cramer's men.'

He rose to his feet.

'Henry's dead,' Saracen told him.

'Figured as much.'

A man appeared, his left arm in a sling. Obviously wounded during the outlaw's rampage. Faraday said to him, 'It is a bad day, Jacob.'

The Choctaw nodded. 'Bad for many of my people, Faraday.'

'And mine. They killed the whole detail, to break Allen free. Dan Bliss is dead.'

'Indeed, a sad day,' Jacob Tall Tree acknowledged.

'What happened?' Saracen asked.

'They came just before dark. Stopped here and

146

shouted for Henry. He came out and *Nanapolo* killed him.'

Saracen frowned. 'Who?'

Faraday said, 'It is a word the Choctaws use for evil spirits. Kinda like the Devil.'

'You mean Allen?' Saracen asked.

'Yes,' said Jacob Tall Tree. 'Henry killed one bad man before he died. I shot one too, before one of them wounded me. They killed Johnny Hawkfeather and many others.'

'What happened to Nita?' the former scout asked.

Jacob stared at the ground and shook his head.

'What happened, Jacob?' Faraday asked.

'Allen had his way with her and then took her with them.'

'When did they leave?' Saracen asked.

'In the middle of the night.'

'Where did they go?'

Jacob shrugged. 'I do not know.'

'Christ,' Faraday snarled.

'But there may be someone who does,' Jacob added.

'Who?'

'They left the wounded man behind.'

Puzzled, Saracen asked, 'Why?'

'He is dying. Won't see out the day.'

'Take us to him, Jacob,' Faraday told him. 'We'll get something out of the bastard.'

Jacob led them to a rundown shack on the edge of town. Outside the door stood a policeman with a Winchester. 'He is in there.'

147

They entered the building, which was little more than a ruin with a collapsing roof, and the first thing that hit them was the smell of the man whose guts were spilling from an open wound. Finch's breathing was laboured, and every now and then he moaned with pain.

'Can you hear me?' Faraday asked the dying man.

He said nothing.

Faraday tried again. 'Hey, can you hear me?'

This time Finch moaned.

'Where is Allen going?'

A moan.

'This is useless,' Faraday complained.

Saracen stepped forward and stared down at Finch. He watched him for a moment and then hit him just below the ribcage.

With a roar of pain, Finch sat up. Saracen grabbed him by his scruffy hair and snarled close to his ear, 'Where's Ted Allen gone?'

Finch stared at him through pain-filled eyes. His breath came in gasps and his mouth opened but nothing came out.

Saracen could see that the man had very little time left. If he didn't extract an answer soon, the man would pass out and never wake up. He asked again, 'Where's Allen?'

'Ka . . . Kansas,' he gasped.

'Where in Kansas?'

But it was no use. The sudden surge of energy brought about by the pain was gone and Finch went limp and remained unresponsive.

Saracen let him go and the outlaw slumped back on the cot.

They returned to the fresh air and sunshine, leaving the man to die in his crumbling coffin. Saracen said, 'I guess we're going to Kansas.'

Nodding, Faraday asked, 'Jacob, can you send word to Marshal Hudgins in Fort Smith? Tell him what has happened and that we're trailing the outlaws.'

'I will have someone leave right away, but just so you know, I'm coming with you.'

The two deputies glanced at each other and then nodded. Faraday said, 'All right. Do what you have to first. We're leaving in an hour.'

CHAPTER 11

South of Muskogee

Bodie sat beside the fire and gave the coals under the coffee pot a stir. Thunder rolled to the west and lightning streaked the sky. Allen came across to him and sat down beside the outlaw. 'You want a cup?' Bodie asked, offering one up.

'Sure.'

Allen took a sip and pulled a face. 'What the hell do you call that?'

'Bad,' Bodie told him.

'I'll say,' Allen agreed. 'Listen, tomorrow I want one of Cramer's men to head into Muskogee.'

Alarm registered on Bodie's face. 'Why?'

'Why do you think?' Allen said.

'Can't we just keep going to Kansas and find a job to do up there?'

'We'll do that too.'

'How about I go? See what I can dig up.'

Allen stared at him for a time and then nodded. 'OK. You go.'

150

Bodie looked across at Nita Grey Elk. In the fire-light, he could see the bruises on her face. He asked, 'What are you going to do with her?'

Allen rubbed at the furrows on his right cheek, courtesy of Nita's nails. 'I aim to keep her for a while. So keep your eyes off her. She's mine.'

Remaining silent, Bodie stirred the coals again.

'Leave in the morning,' Allen ordered. 'Hang around until you find something out, then come back. If you ain't found anything out after a couple of days, come back and we'll keep riding.'

'I still think this is a bad idea, Ted.'

Allen's hard gaze settled on him. 'And I don't care much what you think.'

Another crash of thunder, and then the sky above them opened up.

The overnight storm had washed away any sign the trio had been following, cleansing the land of any-thing obvious. Saracen eased his horse to a stop and muttered under his breath as he looked at the puddles and mud that lay all around. Faraday and Jacob eased in beside him. 'What was that?' Faraday asked him.

'I said this is a waste of damn time,' Saracen growled. 'That bastard rain last night wiped out every-thing.'

Jacob Tall Tree said, 'I'm like you. I've seen nothing.'

'They could have gone in any direction.'

'Well, we know which way they're headed. Maybe we'll get lucky,' Faraday said.

'Let's hope Nita does,' Saracen said grimly.

'We need some extra supplies with Jacob along,' Faraday pointed out. 'How about we swing by Muskogee? Maybe they might have heard something there.'

Saracen said, 'One night. Then we continue.'

'All right.'

It was by pure chance that they stumbled across the outlaws. Riding along, they crested a rise, and before them in a low patch of ground, lay the camp of the men they sought.

'Oh Christ!' Faraday cried out when the outlaws scrambled for their weapons. 'Into them, Blaine! It's Allen!'

Saracen dragged his Schofield from its holster and snapped off a shot at a running figure. The outlaw threw up his arms and fell face down. Blaine didn't know it at the time, but he'd just killed Henshaw.

A slug burned the air close to Saracen's face and he ducked low instinctively. To his right, Faraday was firing his six-gun at the killer known as the Renegade. Over to his left he saw Jacob's horse stumble and fall. A wild-eyed outlaw was standing over him, about to put a bullet in the stunned Choctaw's head.

Saracen fired a shot at him, and by luck more than anything else, the bullet struck the barrel of the six-gun, sending it flying. The outlaw cried out, glanced at the former scout, and started running towards where the horses were tied.

Sighting along the barrel, Saracen was about to

squeeze off a shot when he was heaved from the saddle by Larry Kane. He hit the ground hard beside his horse's prancing hoofs. Kane dived on top of him and clawed at his throat with hooked fingers.

Saracen had lost his grip on the Schofield and bunched his fist. He hit the snarling Kane in the side of his head, but the man hardly budged. He hit him again, and this time the outlaw grunted.

A third blow went wide, and Kane finally got his fingers clamped around Saracen's throat. The pressure was intense, and the former scout could feel his throat being crushed. He scrabbled around in the dirt until his hand found an object that was hard and lumpy. Saracen swung it with brutal force to connect with the side of the outlaw's head.

Kane grunted and went limp. The former scout hit him again to make certain and heard a sickening crunch. He rolled the outlaw off him and groped around for the Schofield.

He found it and came up to his knees, looking for the outlaw who'd run for the horses. When he sighted him, the man was astride and riding hell for leather away from the camp.

'God damn it!' Saracen cursed.

A six-gun cracked close by and he swung about. Faraday had his weapon raised and pointed at the Renegade who was down on his knees, fighting to bring up his own six-gun.

At the top of his voice, Faraday could be heard shouting, 'Don't! Don't!'

But the outlaw was too far gone to hear what was

153

being said, and from pure instinct he kept going.

Faraday squeezed the trigger and the Renegade's shoulders slumped, the six-gun, still in his grip, falling to the ground. His head dropped to his chest, and he toppled over and stopped moving.

Suddenly all was silent. Saracen called over to Jacob. 'Are you all right?'

'I am fine.'

'What about you, Amos?'

'That was wild, Blaine,' the deputy said with a crazy grin. 'Damned wild. That's one way to find the men you're after. It's a shame that Allen got away.'

'The rider?' Saracen asked.

'Yeah.'

The former scout gave the deputy an anxious look. Faraday understood his predicament and said, 'Don't just stand there. Get after him.'

'Blaine!'

Saracen turned to stare at the form of Nita Grey Elk. She was battered and bruised, her clothes torn. 'Nita? Are you OK?'

'I will be fine now that you and Amos are here.'

'I have to go, Nita. I have to get Allen.'

She nodded. 'Yes, kill him.'

'Not before I get some answers.'

Saracen knew that he was getting close. Judging by the trail being left by the horse, he could see that it was tiring. He urged on his own mount until he rounded a turn in the trail – and before him stood Black Ted Allen, afoot and gun raised.

154

The Winchester cracked and spewed forth a puff of blue-grey smoke. The bullet passed close to Saracen with a resounding crack. The former scout hugged the neck of his horse and shouted at the animal: 'Heyaah!'

The horse lunged forwards, and its right shoulder hit the outlaw before he was able to reload and fire. There was a sickening crunch when the animal's hoofs crushed the killer's ribs as it trampled him. When Saracen heard it, he cursed under his breath. He jumped clear of the saddle while the horse was still moving, and ran to the fallen outlaw's side.

Allen was fighting broken ribs which had punctured his lungs. His chest was filling with blood and his lungs wouldn't inflate.

Red fluid was already running from the corner of his mouth.

'Where's my sister?' Saracen snapped. 'What did you do with my sister?'

Allen's eyes flicked back and forth as he tried to comprehend the last moments of his life. The killer smiled, a weak rise of the corners of his mouth. And then the light in his eyes faded, and he died.

Saracen couldn't believe it. He grabbed the lapels of the dead outlaw's coat and shook him violently.

'Damn you, you son-of-a-bitch!' he shouted at him. 'Damn you to bloody hell!'

Muskogee, Creek Nation

They rode into Muskogee with the corpses draped over the trailing horse. The morbid procession drew to a halt outside of a building used by the Creek

Lighthorse. As they dismounted, two policemen emerged and stopped cold. They stared at the sight before them, then one asked, 'What is this, Amos?'

'Black Ted Allen and his boys, Thomas Red Eagle. And those of Hank Cramer. He's dead too.'

'Where did you find them?'

'Not far outside of Muskogee. They hit Anson's Post and killed Henry Grey Elk along with others. They also killed a bunch of marshals including Dan Bliss.'

'That is sad.'

Faraday nodded. 'Yes, but I guess the only up side is that they are all dead.'

The two Creeks glanced at each other and then Thomas said, 'Not quite.'

'What do you mean?' asked Saracen.

'As you know, we're not really allowed to lock up whites. But this morning a man rode into town and he caused trouble with one of the Creek women. So, we locked him up.'

Faraday frowned. 'Who is he?'

'Bodie.'

'Allen's Bodie?'

Thomas nodded.

Faraday looked at Saracen. 'This might be your lucky day.'

The former scout nodded and said, 'Let's go and talk to him.'

Faraday said, 'Thomas?'

'Sure.'

'Jacob, stay with Nita.'

They followed Thomas inside the dimly lit building

and found Bodie in one of two roughly made cells. The other contained the prisoner they were originally to pick up. Bodie saw them and said, 'Thank God you two white men are here. Will you tell them that they can't lock me up like this?'

'We're marshals, Bodie,' Faraday informed him.

His face fell. 'Oh, Christ.'

'Got a feller here who wants to talk to you. And depending on what you say, it could mean the difference of being taken to Fort Smith or back to Anson's Post.'

'You can't do that,' Bodie bleated.

Blaine held out his hand and Thomas gave him the key. He said, 'Maybe not, but I can.'

He opened the door and walked across to the outlaw. Before the cringing figure could do anything, Saracen hit him. Hard.

The former scout stood over him and growled, 'You lot killed a family a while back in Texas, remember?'

'No.'

Saracen hit him again. 'Remember?'

'No.'

Again. 'Remember?'

'Yes! Yes, damn it.'

'They were *my* family.'

'You're him?'

Saracen frowned. 'What?'

'Allen said her brother was looking for her. You're him. Bliss told Ted.'

'I am. Now, where is she? Where's Victoria?'

'I don't know.'

157

Blaine hit him again. 'Where?'

'I don't know. Honest. Allen sold her to Cramer. Cramer sold her to a trader up in Kansas.'

Saracen hit him again harder and cursed him. 'Who, damn it?'

'Cramer didn't say.'

Blaine made to hit Bodie once more but stayed his hand. He knew the outlaw was telling the truth.

Turning to leave the cell, Saracen walked outside, followed by Faraday. The deputy said, 'At least you know she's still alive.'

'But for how long, Amos?'

Faraday shook his head. 'I couldn't say.'

Saracen reached up and unpinned the badge from his shirt. He held it out to Faraday and said, 'I'm done, Amos. I have to head on up to Kansas and see if I can find Victoria.'

The deputy nodded and took it. 'I understand, Blaine. I'll be fine here. Jacob can help me take the prisoners back. You just find your sister.'

Saracen held out his right hand and Faraday took it. 'Been nice working with you, Amos. Take care.'

'You too, Blaine.'

Saracen turned away and was about to mount his horse when a voice said, 'Take me with you, Blaine Saracen.'

He stared at Nita Grey Elk. 'I can't do that, Nita. I don't know what is next for me. Even where I'll be going. Maybe you should go back to Anson's.'

'There is nothing there for me. Henry is dead. I want to come with you. Maybe I can help you find her.'

'No.'

'If you don't take me, I'll follow you.'

By the look in her eyes he knew she would do it. Saracen shook his head and said, 'Well, if you're coming with me, we'll need to get you a few things, including a horse.'

'I'll take one of theirs,' Nita said, nodding at the corpses.

'All right, Nita. Maybe two of us will have more luck than one.'

An hour later the pair rode out of Muskogee, headed north on a search that would take them across the vast expanse of the west.

Fort Smith, Arkansas

The badge landed heavily on the desktop in front of Judge Isaac Parker with a dull thud. He stared at it for a moment and then shifted his gaze to Faraday.

'He's gone,' the deputy said. 'Saracen. He's gone to Kansas. Seems his sister was sold to some trader up there.'

'He couldn't have come back to give me the badge himself?' Parker growled.

'What? And end up being hogtied into something else by you?'

In the corner, Bass Reeves smirked. It wasn't often that one of the marshals stood up to the judge.

'All right. Fine,' Parker grumbled. 'I have another job for you, anyway. You can partner up with Bass. He's headed into the Strip. He'll tell you what he wants.'

'Is that it?' Faraday asked.

Parker put his head down and went back to his writing. 'That's it.'

Both Reeves and Faraday started towards the door.

'And Amos,' Parker said.

Faraday stopped and turned. 'Yeah?'

'I'm sorry about Dan Bliss. I know he was a good friend.'

'Me too, Judge. Me too.'

1	2	3	4	5	6	7	8	9
							8514	